Highway One

Joyce Johnson

A Wings ePress, Inc.
Cozy Mystery

Wings ePress, Inc.

Edited by: Jeanne Smith
Copy Edited by: Melody Bancroft
Executive Editor: Jeanne Smith
Cover Artist: Trisha FitzGerald-Jung

Wings ePress Books
www.wingsepress.com

Published In the United States Of America

Wings ePress Inc.
3000 N. Rock Road
Newton, KS 67114

Dedication

To Jo Ellen Conger, a fellow author at Wings-epress, who not only supports me in my efforts in writing, but who also serves as my mentor.

* * *

One

Driving out of San Francisco on a Friday night isn't easy. When Laura Olsen started her long drive, vehicles were crowding the bridge in both directions. It was a clear day and a mass of tourists was also walking across the Golden Gate Bridge. She crossed over the water with the wind making white caps across the ocean. Postcard perfect, sailboats were swaying in unison against the wind as if on cue. Looking between the large beams of the bridge, she too enjoyed the view.

But just past Sausalito, on her way north, it became monotonous on Highway 101, just cars and mostly level driving. An occasional glimpse of cows grazing punctuated the scene. At the Cloverdale turnoff from Highway 101 to 128, she stopped for a quick snack. June would have a later dinner prepared for her, but she hadn't eaten all day and she was hungry and tired from driving. Even though it was not wise to lose time by stopping to eat, she spotted an intriguing sign proclaiming the world's biggest hamburger, and she wanted to see it. She would get something smaller to eat.

Years ago, the small town of Cloverdale had been bypassed by the revamping of Highway 101. On this piece of the old Redwood Highway, there existed this remnant of bygone days where weary travelers stopped. The inside of the restaurant was as memorable as its rustic log cabin exterior with postcards cluttering the walls. As she waited for her pulled pork sandwich with its secret barbecue sauce, she glanced at some of them.

"Even one from Sean Penn," said the young waitress as she took Laura's order. "We collect as many as we can." She quickly went to the next table without waiting for any comment. The sandwiches looked delicious but larger than anticipated; the restaurant was busy and service was slow. Unavoidably she had spent at least a half hour at the stop. When her order finally came up, Laura left, taking the sandwich with her, regretting that she had stopped at all. Leaving Cloverdale, she began the long, narrow, and winding road through the old farmlands that would be her only companion.

She would straddle the Navarro River through meadows and forests until reaching the connection with Highway One on the Pacific Coast. She would travel through the Anderson Valley with its vineyards and farms. She would also be accompanied by old oaks, chaparral, and grasses until she reached the end near the ocean where redwood forests would engulf her. Remnants of small settlements were strung along the route, including Boonville, which at one time had their own unique slang, and Philo, which now housed only a few buildings. Because of the forests, logging was prevalent in the 1800s as well as farms with sheep and cattle. Fairly well wiped out in the 1940s, wineries had made their appearances again with the first modern one to operate in the 1960s. Laura understood that many wineries dotted Highway 128 through the rolling hillside. *I will have to visit some of them while I am here.*

Rainclouds were gathering overhead, and she again regretted her decision to stop at Cloverdale. She pulled over and called her friend and said she would be later than planned. Laura could hear June's husband in the background grumbling his displeasure, but there was not much she could do to avoid being late. It wasn't long before the heavy rain arrived and with it came more wind. She was very alone on the road, with no street lights to keep her company.

The road was slippery, especially on the hairpin turns and fear crept into her mind as she wound through the hillside. The road swept before her like a bright ribbon in the darkness and she allowed herself to feel the fright. It was delicious in the way it heightened her awareness and awakened her senses. The rain pelted down on the windshield too steadily for the wipers to keep up. The darkness enveloped the landscape around her until the only thing she saw were the shapes of trees as they swept by the fast car, and the road ahead lit by her headlights.

I am the only one on the road, she reminded herself. *What if I miss a turn and crash?* She noticed few farmhouses. For the most part, they were darkened. No one would find her wreck until morning. The headlights would be facing up toward the dark sky, but no one else would notice because no one was coming down the road. She turned up the volume of the local radio station to drown out the voices in her head and sang along loudly, enjoying her freedom and her fear. The local radio station was playing golden oldies from the past, which happened to be Laura's favorite music. She cranked it up even louder as one song from the sixties proclaimed love to be a disaster. That was just her feeling right now, and she happily sang along with the lyrics she knew well.

She might as well enjoy the little sports car now, for before too long it would not be hers. Nor would there be the parties and the expensive clothes that had been part of her persona. She faced a reduced income and the loss of some friends. She would miss the car.

The road continued to bend and twist in a series of turns, occupying more of her thoughts and forcing quick decisions. She felt like she was racing and imagined herself as wild and reckless. Once, on a ski slope she had enjoyed such a moment until a faster skier passed her and the comparison dampened her spirits. Now, as the only person on the road, she could at least enjoy this feeling of speed.

After a seemingly endless number of turns, a flattened countryside emerged dotted with fewer oaks and even fewer farmhouses. This landscape descended into a forest of redwood trees whose canopy eclipsed the moon and brought darkness. The comparison of the two landscapes was startling, and with the looming trees came even more imagined horrors. *Large creatures might be lurking just behind those trees.* She could see there were campsites among the redwoods, but no one was there this night. She continued speeding through the blackness with the radio blaring.

An ad broke into her imaginings and she flipped through the few available stations in search of a tune that matched her spirits but found none. Grudgingly, she turned the radio off and made a note to herself to fix the disc player before she had to relinquish the car. She had to dismiss her fantasies as the bridge would be coming up soon, and the Navarro River, which had been paralleling her journey, would widen and reach the Pacific Ocean. It was at this junction with Highway One she would continue north up the California coast.

She would not be able to see the ocean when she joined Highway One because of the darkness, but knowing it was there just below the rugged cliffs was enough. At the conjunction of Highway One and 128, she continued to the right and swung up to the cliffs joining Highway One. Now the coast was at her left straight down to the ocean. As she continued up the coast on the narrow two-lane road, her ego deflated with the reality that her risky adventure was mostly due to her being late. If she had left San Francisco earlier, and if she had not stopped for a snack, she would not be driving in the dark. To make matters worse, she noticed a car following behind her after only driving a few miles further. Its left headlight was not functioning properly and was dimmed while the other shone brightly in her rearview mirror.

"Great! Now I have a tailgater," she grumbled to herself. "My last few miles in the dark...rainy, late, and on a narrow road on a cliff. I'll spend more time driving with this irritation!" She moved the rearview mirror upwards so the one remaining headlight of the car behind her would not shine in her eyes and possibly better yet, shine on the driver behind her. But at the first small road that appeared to the right, the driver turned off. The car was a small, older, light-colored sedan not worth remembering. Laura was relieved. The rain had stopped, and the last moments' driving were quite ordinary. The road she wanted appeared. She would be at her friend's house soon and was rehearsing her apologies for being late. She thought better of telling June and Stan about having stopped for a snack. Less said the better.

<h1 align="center">*Two*</h1>

June was gracious, but Stan was clearly irritated. They were at the door of the bed and breakfast as Laura drove into their circular driveway. Doubtless they had seen her headlights coming down the narrow road and were waiting to greet her. The house at night looked somewhat like the stern Victorian residence it once had been, but she had no doubt June had made it cheery with ruffles and frills and gingerbread trimmings.

At the door, June looked happy her friend had made it safely, but Stan was grumbling about women always being late. He disappeared right after greeting her with the excuse the two women probably wanted to talk by themselves. Both were relieved when he left the room.

June remarked, "I don't know why he is so grumpy. He sat down to dinner and after you called, he went out to work on his car for a while. He wasn't that inconvenienced."

"Well, again, I am sorry for being late. Now we can catch up on old times if you want to stay up longer," Laura said.

"I haven't been waiting for your visit all day just to go to bed early!" said June. "Let me reheat your dinner, and both of us can enjoy a glass of wine or two. They make excellent organic wines at the local vineyards."

Laura had forgotten how easy it was to talk with June. The years since college evaporated as they caught up with each other and their news. June had married Stan a few years before. She met him through a friend Laura didn't know, so they talked little about his background. Laura told June about her pending divorce and accepted June's condolences and thoughts about her future. June hinted all was not well with the business but would expand on the subject later. She wanted Laura to know it would be easy watching the bed and breakfast for a week as they only had one guest. Her excuse was that it was the beginning of the slow season.

The housekeeper came in a few hours daily to help, so Laura would not have anything to do but supervise her. The housekeeper put out breakfast in the kitchen the night before, and Laura and the one guest were the only ones to serve. It was more enjoyable to talk about old times, so they swapped tidbits from their college days. They continued chatting for another two hours before calling it a night and going to bed. Laura looked around the room after saying goodnight to June and closing her door. Just as she thought, June had decorated the room with a floral theme, including curtains and a matching comforter with lots of pillows on top of the bed. There was a small couch in the room as well.

They had met in college. June belonged to a group of friends more elevated than Laura in social standing and certainly with more money to spend. But after seeing each other in several classes, they finally went out for coffee. At the time they shared little of the same interests or activities, except rating the good-looking men on campus. On that they agreed, except that June talked to a "ten" at least daily, but Laura was not so lucky. Nonetheless, they became friends and, although Laura longed for the other woman's looks and steady supply of money, she liked her honesty and optimism. Laura hadn't seen June for years until that day in San Francisco when she bumped into her at the DeYoung museum. Not surprising because they did have the same taste in art.

On that day, Laura tried her usual tactic of looking down at her shoes and walking quickly, hoping to avoid the other woman altogether. But it hadn't worked as June was too aware of other people for that trick. Laura tried to smile, but just wasn't up to seeing her or hearing about June's perfect life.

"You look great," June had said. "What have you been up to all these years?"

Laura wanted to blurt out that she was going through a divorce and living by herself in San Francisco but soon would have to move out of her apartment. Her biological clock was ticking loudly and when she passed by women pushing baby strollers, Laura found herself weeping. She decided to brag about her career instead.

"I'm just great," she had lied. "I am living in San Francisco and focusing full time on my work."

"Oh," June replied, filling in the blanks, "Are you divorced?"

"Not yet," Laura said, seeing no need to elaborate.

"I only met your husband once, but I'm sure you will find someone better," she said. "How about lunch? Have you eaten? This museum has a great restaurant!" June dragged her long-lost friend into the restaurant and so the two were reunited.

To her relief, Laura was able to appreciate her friend. June showed her a photo of Stan (a ten, of course), but when Laura found out June didn't have kids, she relaxed a bit. June said she and her husband had decided to cash in their investments (and of course her parents pitched in) and bought a B & B in Mendocino a year before. But neither had it been as fun or as profitable as they anticipated. There were lots of expenses at first and lots of competition locally. Yet they loved the area and were trying to make a go of it.

"Why don't you come and visit us?" June asked.

"I think I might feel uncomfortable with all those romantic couples gazing at each other over breakfast."

"Then why don't you housesit for a week—free of course—and you won't be a guest, just a friend visiting a friend. Light chores and a good reason to be in Mendocino and not as a romantic getaway. I think you will like the village and the people who live there. Since you will be working and not a tourist, you can view the village differently."

June was quite convincing as always, and the more she talked, the more Laura pictured herself relaxing at a B & B. It was tempting. So they agreed on a date, and Laura found herself daydreaming at work about her profile against the foggy mists of Mendocino with a freshly painted white Victorian in the background. Finally, she was there.

Laura slid into the cool sheets of her overstuffed bed initially surrounded by masses of pillows that she removed and put on chairs. It was good to feel safe and protected, and she told herself to enjoy the pampering. June and Stan were off for the week after attending the wedding of June's cousin in Santa Rosa, a town south of them. The two would be staying at a B & B nearby whose owners they both knew and respected and hoped might give them some ideas about how to improve their business.

Laura thought about her little adventurous drive and how it concluded with a warm, safe bed. As she lay under the covers, exhausted by her long drive, she fell asleep, content in her security. It was not until the next morning that she learned what had happened the previous night.

Three

When she awoke, all was silent in the large house, and Laura wondered at the hour and how long she had slept. Reassured by her watch it was still early, she showered quickly and put on jeans and a sweatshirt before wandering through the old house. June had told her the old Victorian had been converted into a bed and breakfast by the previous owners. When viewed by them and the realtor, June and Stan had considered themselves lucky to find a house that had been already renovated. The previous owners had not only updated the second-floor bedrooms with bathrooms, but they had converted a sun room and a parlor on the first floor into additional bedrooms for guests who didn't want to or couldn't climb stairs. The previous owners were going to install a hot tub on the grounds of the inn, but they had run out of money.

June and Stan had found out from the realtor that not only had the owners ran out of money, but they had never booked all the rooms...never. When Laura heard this from June, she was concerned. Apparently, June and Stan were not, and bought the converted

Victorian property. June spent lavishly refurbishing the rooms to her taste, while Stan happily spent money putting in a hot tub and a surrounding garden.

Laura preferred staying on the bottom floor with easy access so she would not have to climb the stairs each day. The lodger had requested the first floor as well, and Laura thought this was handy, as she could keep an eye on his needs.

Laura went upstairs and peeked into the other bedrooms. As Laura had predicted, June had filled them with pastel colors. There was flowery wallpaper in each bedroom and lots of matching comforters and pillows. Each bedroom looked out to either the front yard or the back garden. She heard the lowered voices of Stan and June as she walked back down the stairs. As Laura approached, she wondered at the secrecy. Pouring herself a cup of hot coffee, she could now make out what they were saying.

"I can't believe she is missing," said June. "Would she really run away?"

"She was probably unhappy. Why would that be surprising?" returned Stan.

Curious, Laura lingered at the doorway, hoping to catch more phrases. Instead, June and Stan spied her presence and invited her to join them. They ended their conversation and just spoke to her about trivial matters.

"Did you have a good night's sleep?" asked June.

Stan moved toward the kitchen counter and pointed to the coffeepot. "There is plenty of coffee," he said. "I have to drive into town for a few things. Do you want me to pick up anything for either of you?"

"No thanks," said June. "I went into town yesterday and have plenty of supplies."

Then, as if to tell June something in a coded way, Stan said to her, "I'll get more news about what we were discussing." He left the kitchen abruptly, swinging the screen door hard behind him. He seemed angry, and Laura wondered if he was still mad at her for being late the previous evening.

"I heard you talking as I came in," said Laura. "Is it local gossip?"

June turned her face away and lowered her voice as if it were a secret and there were others in the room.

"A friend of mine, a woman I know through our local business association, has disappeared. She and her husband own a bed and breakfast inn near where the Navarro River flows out under the bridge leading to the ocean. The sheriff called this morning and told us her husband reported her missing. He wanted to know if we knew anything."

"Well, do you?" Laura asked, letting curiosity dominate discretion.

"Not really," June answered. She looked down again and spoke once more in a secretive voice. "And I didn't mention this to the sheriff, but she recently shocked me at a party when she boasted about the possibility of leaving her husband. I dismissed it at the time, and I thought she was joking and it was a result of her drinking. She always drank a lot."

"Let's eat breakfast outside on the porch," she said, changing the subject. "Afterwards, I want to show you the garden and then I'll take you on a tour of the house. Our one guest has finished his breakfast, and the housekeeper, Mrs. Evans, has left. We will have the run of the place until Stan gets back. Let's enjoy ourselves."

They joined arms as the pals they once were, and June brought a breakfast tray with croissants and hot coffee to the porch where they ate and chatted about absolutely nothing while enjoying each other's company. They left their dishes there and June led Laura into the crowded garden of colorful annuals and perennials.

"Are you the gardener? This is absolutely beautiful," said Laura.

"Heavens no! We hired someone from the village. I can't include gardening as one of my talents, but I did decorate the interior myself."

They returned to the porch, and Laura disappeared inside the inn with the dishes and brought back some more hot coffee. They sat for a while longer and talked. Time was forgotten. When Stan's car appeared at the entrance of the long driveway, Laura found herself just as disappointed as June appeared to be. He joined them on the porch but brought little news of the woman's disappearance.

"Well," Stan barked, "did you tell Laura what she needs to know to run the place for a week? I'm anxious to leave right after breakfast tomorrow."

She and June had not discussed one item about running the bed and breakfast, so Laura answered with the tact she had developed during her now-defunct marriage while trying to keep the peace. Stan was like her husband in the sense that he really didn't want honesty. He only wanted the right answers.

"We have some details yet to discuss, and everything will be in order before you leave," Laura told him, avoiding any further discussion by asking him questions about the town. June threw her a grateful glance.

"Is the sheriff a good resource should I have any problems?" Laura asked.

"Not really," answered Stan. "He usually doesn't have much to do. Spends a lot of time talking to people in town...mostly women. Besides, you won't have any problems you need to worry about. After you make sure our guest has his breakfast and you have made conversation with the housekeeper, you are free to enjoy shopping in the village. June certainly does just that."

"Thanks," said Laura.

Stan excused himself again and went off somewhere. Laura wrinkled her nose and thought, *I wish I had more time to spend with my friend.* But at least she had one more evening with her.

Four

At dinner that night, there was no more discussion about the missing woman, and it didn't feel appropriate for Laura to ask. June filled her in about such details as changing linens. Their lodger didn't want anyone in his room and told them when the Mrs. Evans could change sheets and towels as well as prepare breakfast and snacks in the morning to put in the refrigerator. He paid for a month, kept to himself and was gone a lot. Often, he left with some expensive binoculars, so they concluded he must be a birdwatcher.

June alluded that their business was less than lucrative, but she still felt optimistic. Stan was more pessimistic about their chance of succeeding, and hence they needed a break to discuss their plans and hoped this couple with whom they were staying had some fresh ideas.

The next morning the two left the house before breakfast. After talking with the Mrs. Evans, Laura decided to make a trip into the small town and acquaint herself with the surroundings. June had marked all the small shops and places to eat on the town's brochure.

As the bed and breakfast was only a short distance from the town, Laura drove on Highway One with the Pacific Ocean at her side. As she turned a corner on the two-lane road, a view of the headlands lay ahead of her like the cover on a travel magazine. Dotted with historic buildings and water towers from the 1860s, the view was a great photo opportunity and she would return to take one herself. She made a curved left into town after crossing the bridge over yet another river. Laura headed straight for Mimi's Cheese and Wine Shop that June had recommended. She would pick up some snacks for a nice evening meal on the porch.

She parked near the Masonic Hall, a landmark from the 1870s, with its statue of Father Time on the roof proudly surveying the village. According to June, the statue had nothing to do with Father Time at all, but instead belonged to Masonic rituals. Carved out of a solid block of redwood, the statue's true meaning was known only to Masons who had sold the first floor to a bank many years earlier, but still held meetings on the second floor. Another mystery in this small village.

The town itself, according to June, was no larger than four or five blocks each way...easy walking for Laura. It was filled with little shops on each street and Laura was anxious to discover each of them. She opened the door of Mimi's Wine and Cheese Shop with the jingle of the bells, but no one seemed to notice. There were half a dozen people inside, mostly women. The shop was decorated with white lacy curtains and furnished with made-to-look-like antique ice cream parlor tables and chairs. Each chair featured cozy cushions on the seats and backs. The bakery case was filled with all kinds of croissants, cupcakes, and muffins. In addition, there were many varieties of cookies displayed and the hand-lettered menu on the wall listed several options for drinks, including organic teas and coffees.

Laura noticed the only male customer wore a sheriff's badge. She ordered a local red wine from the Navarro winery and some brie that paired well with it for her evening snack on the porch. She sat down with a cup of coffee on a neighboring table to eavesdrop. The conversation centered on the woman who had disappeared. The sheriff was asking the group of women sitting together if they knew anything.

Laura doubted they would tell him, even if they knew anything personal about the missing woman. However, he seemed to know all of them well and chatted on about other happier events in town until his cell phone interrupted. The sheriff excused himself, saying he was needed elsewhere and tipped his hat to the ladies as he left. Laura lingered after his departure and initiated a conversation with a woman wearing a handmade shawl at the table with the other women adjoining hers.

"That is a beautiful scarf," said Laura.

"Thank you," the woman replied. "Why don't you join us?"

Laura moved over to the group, ordering more coffee and a croissant.

"You must be the friend June told us about," said another.

"How did you know?" asked Laura.

"June described you and said you might be coming here as she suggested. June came in as often as she could, but never talked much. When she did engage in conversation, she usually grumbled about her husband. By the way, the lady who owns the beautiful scarf is Sheila." She pointed to her at the table. "She recently moved here and bought the jewelry shop a block from here," the woman said.

"Lucky June can get away from the inn for a while," said another.

"Do you also own a B & B?" Laura asked the woman who asked her to join them.

"No, I am the local realtor. My name is Julie, and if you become interested in staying, I can help you find a place to rent...or buy. People who visit often come back and buy or rent something in town. Take my card," she said, handing Laura her business card without waiting for her to agree.

"Sounds like your little town has some excitement going on right now," said Laura.

Julie looked at her for a moment, sizing up the situation, and added more.

"Hopefully she has gone off somewhere and will call or come back shortly. The sheriff probably doesn't know this, but Donna has not been herself lately. She talked of leaving town but never gave any details. We think maybe she is having an affair," she whispered, although only the women and the shop owner were there.

After coffee with the ladies, Laura left to visit more of the town. Picking up another local town map at the shop, Laura continued walking around the small village. She stopped at the candle shop and bought some tapers as a present for June. She even found a shawl, like the one Sheila was wearing, at a shop in an old water tower and bought some fresh fruit at the only large grocery store in town.

It seemed a pleasant town, with lots of side streets to explore. The store owners were friendly and helpful, and she could have easily stayed all day. She made a mental note about the stately old hotel on the main street that included a restaurant and a bar. Across the street from the hotel was the state park headquarters where she could get information about the various trails along the headlands leading down to another wide beach. But it was time to go back to the inn as she had been gone several hours.

Upon returning, she noticed a man leaving the inn. He was probably their lone boarder and was apparently taking a walk. Strange time for bird watching, she thought. Her birder friends who asked her to accompany them on day trips usually went out early in the morning. She looked around the inn, but there was nothing to keep her inside. She had brought a new novel and gave it a try on the front porch with no success. She was too distracted by the beauty of the landscape. The ocean beckoned her, so she picked up her map and went walking down the inn's narrow road, which led downhill to Highway One. The traffic was scarce once more, so she crossed the highway easily and within minutes found a path to the beach below. The rock-strewn path was well worn but steep and she watched her steps carefully. Small rocks spewed out from her steps. No one knew she was there if she should fall. The beach itself, when she reached it, was composed of very fine sand and was very lengthy in both directions. It stretched out in a long line as did the rhythmic waves that lapped the shore. Sets of waves continued out in the distance and after that, the ocean was flat. There were no strong storms visible on the horizon, just a few drifting clouds overhead to break up the clear blue sky.

Kelp and driftwood lined the beach from the waves, creating patterns from their emergence from the sea. Laura wandered through the piles looking for treasures that she would take back with her and found a heart-shaped stone and a weathered piece of wood shaped somewhat like a fish. She looked for beach glass, but there didn't seem to be any. The tide was high and she walked easily on the wet sand at the edge of the water as the crashing waves played tag with her.

It was a weekday and off season, and she didn't see any beachgoers. She enjoyed the seclusion as she glanced down the beach in both directions from her starting point at the base of the path. It seemed very peaceful there, just what she needed for some silent meditation. Her cares floated away in the waves, and at least temporarily, she let go of them.

This is what I pictured myself doing, she thought. *What an ideal spot for relaxing. No cares following me.* Reluctantly, she walked back up the narrow path and crossed the highway to return to the inn. It was nearing four o'clock. Although her boarder didn't require company or dinner, June had said Laura should be visible at dinnertime a few times. As she approached the circular driveway, Laura saw the sheriff's car parked in front. Nervous because of her absence, she hoped nothing had happened to the boarder while she was gone.

The sheriff turned from the door and announced his presence. "My name is Jim Clark and I am the sheriff of this county. I understand you are watching the inn while June and Stan are away for a week. Didn't I see you at the wine and cheese shop earlier today?"

Pretty observant, Laura thought. "Anything wrong, Sheriff?"

"Well, I guess you heard from the women at the shop that someone is missing. I couldn't reach your cell phone, so I came in person to inform you and to see if you or your guests have heard or seen anything that would help my search," he said.

Laura winced at the comment about the cell phone. She should have taken the one June had given her to use while they were away.

"No, I haven't heard or seen anything. I have only been here a short time. The inn only has one boarder currently, but when I see him, I will ask," she replied.

"Only one guest?" he asked. "That's too bad. Well, an easy job for you. When you come into town next, look me up. I can tell you about our village and its attractions." Smiling broadly, he emphasized the last two words, and Laura decided he was including himself.

"I might just do that, Sheriff," she countered. "It would be nice to have someone to count on."

"Great. I look forward to it." He ambled down the porch steps, taking his time. He tipped his hat as he waved goodbye before getting into the patrol car.

Seems like that is part of his act. What a showoff, but good looking...tall and fit with wisps of wavy brown hair hidden under his hat.

The guest appeared in the hallway looking worried.

"What did the sheriff want?" he asked with no introduction.

Laura turned around to speak with him.

"He wanted to know if we had heard or seen anything unusual the last two days. A woman was reported missing by her husband," she said.

"What woman?" he asked.

Laura grimaced and inwardly thought, *Why does he want to know that?* but she answered him anyway. "I really don't know her last name, but her first name is Donna."

The lodger stepped back in surprise and seemed visibly upset. He didn't speak for a few seconds, and Laura took that opportunity to figure out her next response.

"They think she probably took off and will return in a few days, so they aren't that worried," she said.

The man muttered something and headed toward his room.

"If you need anything, please tell me," she called out feebly. "My name is Laura, and I am sure June told you I will be taking care of the B & B for the next week."

My only guest and I botched it, she thought.

Laura turned to food for diversion as she always did and fixed some brie on a platter and poured herself some chardonnay. She sat in the stereotypical big white rocking chair on the front porch and soothed herself, looking out into the ocean, the distant horizon, and the endless play of the clouds. The wine started to take effect and, feeling better, she returned to the house and lit a warm fire. The guest never came out of his room although he had kitchen privileges for fixing a snack or getting himself a glass of wine. Laura was relieved he didn't appear again and turned in early with her thoughts clouded with the day's events.

Five

Laura set her alarm clock for early morning so she could meet the part time housekeeper. She found the older woman in the kitchen fixing coffee and checking the food in the refrigerator.

"Good morning," she said.

Mrs. Evans was dressed in a striped, faded dress. She wore flat, comfortable shoes with socks showing beneath her dress. Frumpy, with her mousy brown hair pulled back in a bun, she eyed Laura up and down before she answered.

"Good morning. I understand you're in charge for this week," she said.

"June explained the routine here and it sounds like you already have your duties well under control," said Laura.

"Not much work," she said. "Currently only one guest. Don't know if I'll be here long."

"I know June is pleased with you," said Laura.

"Of course, but she needs more guests. Bad time to leave the inn. She should be looking for more guests," the woman grumbled.

Not wanting to argue, Laura just nodded and poured herself some coffee. "Do you serve coffee to the guest?" she asked, even though she knew the answer. Laura wanted to get some information on the man who shared the house with her at night.

"No. He keeps to himself. Strange, though, when I was cleaning his room on the only day he allows, I found something odd in his trash. The small scrap of paper had clung to the side of the wire waste paper basket and I guess he didn't realize it was left there. So I read it," she freely admitted.

"What was strange about that?" she asked.

"The name and address of the missing woman were written on that paper," Mrs. Evans replied.

"Oh," said Laura. "Maybe he knew her."

"Seems so, but it's the address of the missing woman who is a local. She and her husband own an inn here," said the housekeeper, and turning to finish her duties, signaled the end of the conversation.

That information about the note was rather unnerving. Mrs. Evans had said the missing woman owned the inn off Highway One at the mouth of the Navarro River, so Laura returned to her room for her map to take a drive there. Curious, Laura decided to check out the beach in front of the inn instead of returning to the beach across the road from Stan and June's B & B.

The mouth of the Navarro River was only a few miles south from where she was staying on Highway One, but Laura had difficulty finding the small, narrow road leading away from the highway down to the inn itself. When she found the inn's sign, it pointed to an even smaller dirt road that wound up at the beach. *Out of the way, yet an intriguing location and easy access to the ocean,* Laura thought.

After parking at the inn, she walked down to the beach where she found some teenagers who she figured should be in school. They were making teepees out of the large dry driftwood lying on the beach. Finding it harder to communicate with teenagers rather than women like herself, Laura waited on the sand for an opportunity. She hoped one of them might become curious and talk with her. Finally, one girl walked over to her.

"Are you visiting our town?" the teenager asked.

"Yes," Laura replied. "I'm watching Stan and June's inn for the week while they get away for a while."

"Oh," said the girl and started to walk away.

Laura wanted to engage her in conversation, so she spoke loudly to the parting girl. "I heard about the missing woman who is June's friend. Is that her bed and breakfast up there?" Laura asked, pointing to the inn up from the beach.

"Sure is," said the girl, turning to face Laura. "The town thinks she ran away with someone. We found a note which we gave to the sheriff. It was crumpled and soiled but easy to find. It was signed Donna."

"What did it say?" Laura asked.

"You seem awfully curious? Did you know her?"

"No, I didn't know her, but Stan and June are away, and I wanted to tell them what was going on in town when they come back or if they should call. Have you seen Donna at the beach often?"

"Yes, but not with anyone we know during the daytime, or at least she was way down the beach, and we couldn't tell if it was her, or who she was with either. She didn't talk with us usually. Sheriff Clark has asked us about her since she disappeared. Sometimes on the weekend, we have seen a couple way down on the beach in the evenings, but it was too dark to recognize anyone."

"I spotted a house higher than their inn that looks down on them. Who owns it?"

"That house belongs to Larry Stedman, our local mechanic. He owns the only gas station and auto shop in town. You may not have noticed it, but it's on the main street as you head into the village. Been there forever. His dad owned it and the house long before he was even born. He has lived there all his life and went to the local high school. Never married and after his parents died has lived there alone. No one has been inside for many years. A real odd guy," she said and shook her head as if to say he was creepy.

"Thanks for the local news," Laura said and went back to sitting on the beach.

"No problem," said the girl. "It's the biggest news this town has had since I can remember." She walked back to join her friends.

Laura thought, *she stopped over here to see me. I guess she just wanted to check me out.*

Laura had brought along her cell phone and earplugs for listening to her favorite oldies. In their last big fight, her husband had called her quirky, old-fashioned, and worst of all, not relevant.

"Just like you," he had chided her. "Living in the past and not keeping up with the times."

But she liked her old tunes, and some were still popular. Anyway, they were a comfort since her father played such music constantly when she was growing up. Her mother died when she was very young, and her father did his best to raise her. Sometimes at night after dinner when he was playing his favorites, they would dance in the living room. *These are some of my favorite memories*, she thought. *I don't care that my soon-to-be-ex-husband doesn't approve. I don't approve of all the goofy activities he absorbs himself in to keep himself busy.*

Yet another blast from the past blared forth on the local radio and enlivened Laura's spirits. The tune revolved around a run-around gal. *How appropriate*, she thought. *It reminds me of Donna, who probably did run around too much.*

Laura kept listening as she climbed back up the trail and drove back to the inn. She was surprised to see Stan and June's car in the driveway. When she entered the inn, she found Stan holding golf clubs.

"What's up?" she asked.

Stan said he had forgotten his clubs, and since they were staying at an inn not too far away, he decided to come back and get them. He didn't seem interested in engaging in any conversation, and Laura wasn't eager to talk with him anyway. Maybe his golfing partner was waiting. Stan didn't even ask how everything was working out with her house sitting.

After Stan had driven away, Laura tried again to get interested in the new book she had brought with her, but she couldn't seem to concentrate. She went into her bedroom and thought of the dress she brought with her in hopes of going out one evening. She had found it in San Francisco at a little shop featuring long, Victorian-style dresses. Looking into the full-size mirror, she thought her weight loss during the divorce had served her well as she fit into a smaller size than usual. With the new wraparound shawl thrown casually over her long dress, she walked out. She left a note for the boarder, knowing he probably was not going to read it.

Her destination was dinner at the old Victorian Mendocino Hotel on Main Street, which featured gilded décor with an antique bar and a stained-glass chandelier. She would treat herself to a big, juicy steak, the kind she would have never ordered with her soon-to-be-ex-husband who favored more healthy menus. A glass of an expensive local red wine was just what she needed. Parking would be easy this time of year as the town was not crowded with tourists.

Dating from the 1860s, the two-story faded yellow wooden building oozed antique charm. As she walked into the entrance of the hotel, Laura surveyed its old flavor. Guests sitting in overstuffed chairs enjoyed their glasses of wine in the dark interior of the lobby. Laura had made a reservation but could tell it was not needed. She was seated in the newer dining room down a few steps from the older antique bar adjoining the hotel's living room. She looked around at the few guests. She perused the menu and when she looked up, Laura spotted the sheriff at the top of the stairs chatting with one of the waitresses. Looking back at her menu, Laura was hoping he wouldn't see her, but he spied her and walked over to say hello. When he suggested joining her for dinner, Laura couldn't think of a good excuse for not inviting him and reluctantly relinquished her cherished image of a dinner by herself in a Victorian setting.

"Any news about the missing woman?" she asked.

Clark's face clouded over, and he answered in hushed tones, "It will be in the local paper tomorrow anyway, so I might as well tell you now. Her body was discovered washed ashore at a beach late this afternoon. I informed her husband of the discovery and he seemed devastated."

"Oh," Laura replied. "How terrible. Did she drown? Was it an accident?"

"I won't know until the autopsy, which the local coroner will conduct tomorrow. But I think it was both. Perhaps she was taking a long walk on the beach, fell and hit her head and the tide took her out. That's my guess."

"What a tragedy," Laura replied and thought about her solitary walk on the beach.

"Yes. Sorry to bring this up at your first dinner out. Let me help you with the menu," he said.

"I already know what I want," Laura said, somewhat perturbed at his behavior. "But you can suggest some areas to visit while I'm here. June only has the one boarder and he's a loner...doesn't want any help, and I have time on my hands."

"I would like to show you around, but I'll be very busy in the next few days. For sure you should see the usual sights. There are numerous walks along the headlands beginning at the visitor center just across from the hotel and you can reach the beach where the Big River enters the ocean from one of these trails. You also should visit the art center and maybe take in a show at our local theatre. And of course, just walking on any beach is desirable," he said.

"I already walked the beach today where the Navarro River meets the ocean," Laura said.

"Why did you go there?" he asked.

"I don't know. I wanted to see the inn where the woman lived. June had spoken of it."

"Well, I wouldn't go there again," he said curtly. "Not a good idea."

Just then the waitress brought the wine. "I hear they found Donna's body at the Navarro River beach," she said. "We all thought she ran away with someone." With that comment, the waitress walked away from the table.

Clark's cell phone jingled a tune and he answered in terse tones. "Yes. All right. I'll come over. I'm on my way."

He flagged the waitress back to tell her he wasn't ordering. He turned to Laura and said, "Sorry I have to leave. I'll take a rain check on dinner together." He left without giving Laura a chance to decline his invitation.

At least, thought Laura, *I am back to my solo fantasy in a Victorian hotel. Dining alone in my long, flowered dress and new shawl, I am again free to fantasize about being back in time waiting for someone special to join me.*

After dinner, Laura briefly sat at the bar and enjoyed an after-dinner drink. She couldn't help but admire the Tiffany-style, stained glass dome that hung over the bar as well as the leaded windows and oriental rugs that added to the Victorian charm. The bartender's name was Eric, but the dreamlike sequence was wearing thin, so she walked out in the cool evening to her car that was parked on Main Street in front of the visitors' center. It was late, and the moon shone brightly against a few clouds. She would visit this center tomorrow and perhaps walk some of the trails starting from the headlands.

Six

After speaking to the housekeeper the next day, Laura left and drove into the village to retrieve the inn's mail at the post office. She picked up only bills and advertisements, nothing else of any import. There were no requests for rooms. Next to the post office was the office of the local paper. On the newsstand was the day's edition. She read the headlines and the main story was the woman's body washing up on the shore. She bought one and decided she would read it later. She headed for the visitors' center on Main Street. It was more of a museum, with exhibits concerning the local history of the area. There she picked up another map and decided to take one of the trails leading to the beach below. Winding through the scraggly ocean-swept bushes to the edge of the headlands was rough going, and she turned back to walk to the street when she realized the trail she was on led up to the auto repair shop on Main Street.

She made a quick decision. She wanted to see if the man who owned the shop was there. She was curious about him and what he looked like. So she walked back on the trail to her car and drove it over to the shop. Parking outside, she walked hesitantly inside the old building crowded with discarded car parts and cans. The smell of rancid oil assaulted her senses. Indeed, the building had been there a long time and interestingly enough, it probably had the best view of the ocean from its greasy windows.

The building wasn't on any of the maps, not even on the one listing all the businesses in town. As she entered the building that was open and filled with two cars the mechanics were working on, a young man asked what she wanted. Laura pretended her car had problems when driving that morning. Inside the dilapidated office was exactly the person who the teenager had described as an older unkempt man with stringy hair and some well-worn clothes. He was arguing loudly with another man in the room. The teenager on the beach was right in her assessment. He looked like quite a character.

Her stare must have caught his attention, and Laura turned her head away when he stared back. He told the man he was arguing with to wait in his office and came out to confront her.

"Can I help you with something?" he asked.

"I...I..." she stammered. "I had trouble with my car this morning and wanted to check it out," she lied.

"Anything wrong with her car?" he asked the mechanic who had the hood of Laura's sports car open.

"No. It's a nice clean engine. A beautiful car. Wish it was mine," the guy remarked.

The owner kept silent for a few seconds, eying Laura all the while.

"Guess it's okay. Are you staying in Mendocino long?" he asked. "I spotted your car parked near my house and I saw you walking to the beach. It's a nice sports car. Yours?"

"It belongs to me and my husband," Laura said implying her husband was with her in Mendocino. "Thanks for checking it out."

"Husband not good with cars?"

"No. He's a businessman. Thanks again. I must go. I am meeting him for lunch," she lied and walked straight to the door without looking back. *That man is just creepy.*

Deciding she needed a cup of coffee, maybe with some brandy in it, Laura walked a block to Mimi's Wine and Cheese Shop. Maybe she would buy a small bottle of brandy at the grocery store down the street, but for now a good strong cup of coffee would do. She was shaken by the encounter with the owner of the auto shop. She went inside the cheese shop and was relieved to see the same women as before already there. Mimi, the owner of the shop, joined the group while standing near them to greet other customers if they came in. *Apparently, the group meets daily at the same time and probably has the shop to itself. This time,* Laura thought, *I would like to get to know them better.*

Julie introduced them, giving each one a position in the village. "This is Roberta," Julie said smiling, as she pointed to the newly coiffed, curly-haired brunette seated next to her. "The reason she looks so good is she owns and operates the only beauty shop in town."

"Thanks for the compliment, Julie," the woman responded. "If you stay long enough, do come in and visit me. I could give you some new ideas for your long hair." She cupped her hands beneath her hair and Laura unconsciously did the same with hers. "I have some good products too."

"Always selling herself," laughed Julie. "A good business-woman." Gesturing to the others, she said, "We represent the only businesswomen in town. This is sort of our support group."

"And this is Annie," she said, nodding her head to indicate the woman sitting across from her who looked as though she had never visited a hairdresser. Her long, stringy brown hair fell down her back haphazardly. She wore a long cotton dress recalling the happier days of the 60s and finished the ensemble off with, of course, big flat well-worn sandals.

"Annie owns the natural food store a block over. You must have seen it. Jars and jars of herbs, lots of candles and crystals of all sorts, local organic produce, and all kinds of other natural food items. She gives us advice all the time about our eating habits," said Julie.

"I only drink organic tea in here, "Annie said good-naturedly. "And I haven't given up just yet on converting them from consuming too much sugar."

"Well, this other lady here sells me her cookies and candy," chimed in Mimi. "You have her to thank for your daily sugar intake." She pointed to the last woman at the table. "Sarah owns the Village Cookies and Candy gift shop on Main Street. Tourists like to nibble on something while shopping."

"Laura, did you hear about their finding Donna's body at the mouth of the Navarro River?" Mimi asked, interrupting the introductions with her news.

"Yes, I did," answered Laura. "So much for her running off with some man."

"We were all wrong," said Julie. "She must have been taking a walk on the beach and fell. Probably troubled with a lot on her mind. Even with a full moon, it's difficult to walk on the beach at night. Lots of large driftwood and boulders on that beach."

"What a sad thing to happen. Nobody to help her when she needed it," Roberta commented. "I hope it was an accident and not murder. Bad for business."

"What a thing to say," responded Annie in a sharp tone. "Have some compassion!"

"Well, if she was murdered, there are lots of suspects," replied Roberta.

"Who?" Julie asked.

Mimi jumped into the conversation. "Are you kidding? Lots of women disliked her for flirting with their husbands. Her husband didn't like it. Why she even unmercifully teased Larry at the auto shop. That guy gives me the creeps!"

"He needs a good haircut," offered Roberta.

"He needs more than that. He needs a good shower, new clothes, and a new attitude," answered Julie.

"I just had a run-in with Larry at his auto body shop. There is something weird about that man. Not only does he give off a foul odor, but he looks mean with those piercing black eyes and offensive stare," said Laura. They all cringed a little.

"Odd since he was a child, I hear," said Roberta. "Seems no one liked him in school, but he stayed here anyway and inherited his mother and father's house as well as the business when they died. Rarely comes into town other than to his shop, and he doesn't mix with the other locals. The teenagers on the beach tease him when they see him spying on them from his porch with his binoculars. Donna used to taunt him by pulling up the top of her shirt to reveal herself when he was watching the beach."

"What a thing to say," remarked Annie.

"Even Jim Clark himself is a suspect in a way," whispered Julie. "They went together in high school and her husband was jealous of the sheriff, who also flirts with everybody. Folks say those two were seen in a fight outside the hotel bar a couple of weeks ago."

"Really?" asked Laura.

"It was quite a fight," replied Julie.

They continued chatting for a while about other subjects until another woman joined the group. *Stunning*, Laura thought. She was a tall, thin, long-haired brunette with sharp features like a model. Laura remembered her name was Sheila and when she met her for the first time she was wearing a handmade scarf. When the others had introduced her, they had mentioned she moved there only recently and bought a small jewelry store on a side street of the village.

When she excused herself to return to her shop, the other women joined in, telling Laura Sheila was one of the sheriff's latest conquests. They had been seen several times around town and nobody was surprised at the twosome. Laura kept her almost-dinner date with Clark to herself.

Laura left soon after as she knew they wouldn't be offering any more gossip about the sheriff. Laura had learned of the local theater company, which had been producing plays since the 70s and wanted to see where it was located. The theater was not listed in the brochures Laura was collecting for guests at the B & B, but Julie had recommended to Laura that she check it out. She told her the plays were supported by locals who starred in them but over the years had become more professional, and the playhouse had attracted more interest than just with the locals. Tourists were vocal in their praise.

She wandered over to the theater and checked out the latest offering. The box office was closed, but she noted the phone number. The theater was located next to the art center, and she found herself admiring the various exhibits. The sculpture garden particularly impressed Laura. According to the greeter at the small museum, the outside sculpture garden had been created by a local artist whose bronze bust was located at the entrance to the courtyard. Many sculptures and artists' studios surrounded the courtyard.

Laura learned from the woman that artists and would-be artists displayed their creations in juried events throughout the years. She was impressed by the work and the posters indicating the art center held various showings, conferences, and workshops. Not an artist herself, but an admirer, Laura felt a connection with this place...even more so than the museums in San Francisco.

Morning turned into afternoon, and Laura decided not to linger in the village any longer. She drove back to the inn and found herself deciding to take another look at the beach at the mouth of the Navarro River where she had been yesterday. Although the sheriff seemed unhappy about her going there, she would go anyway. She was tired of any man telling her what to do.

When she returned to the inn, no one was there. No one had even called. She wondered if June and Stan had stopped advertising. In the time she had been there, not one new reservation was made, and June hadn't even called to see if there were any. The housekeeper left a short note to that effect. There was an automated reply if someone did call, and a message would be left on the machine.

The lodger's car was gone again, so she drove down to the path leading to the Navarro River beach. This time she noted the path was located only a short distance from the road where the car tailgating her on Highway One had turned off that first evening. She parked her car and, curious, instead of walking down to the beach she walked to the road leading away from the ocean. There were a few houses located on the street far apart from each other, and it seemed the road continued for quite a distance. Walking back to her car, Laura wondered if she should mention to Clark what she had seen that first night, since it was about the same time as the woman had gone missing. She decided against it. Maybe it was not important.

When she got back to the inn, there was a message from the sheriff taking her up on his "rain check" for dinner. She hesitated but decided she wanted more information on the missing woman, so she called him back and accepted. When they talked on the phone, Laura asked about the restaurant he suggested. She had not heard of it.

"Not on all the brochures because it doesn't need to advertise. Café Beaujolais is upscale for Mendocino. Been here since the 70s with its owner loving the coast and the little village. She was the inspiration for buying an eighteen-hundreds farmhouse and turning it into a destination. She loved the garden and filled it with antique roses and edible plants she used in her cooking. Just your kind of place—an old Victorian farmhouse. It would match your dress," he laughed.

Laura frowned. *Just like him*, she thought.

When they arrived at the little yellow farmhouse near Main Street, she was not disappointed. The garden made the one at the inn look unfinished in comparison with the abundance of roses and tall flowering plants keeping company with each other. The white picket fence surrounding the restaurant finished off the scene, which was made even more romantic with twinkling lights hanging from the trees that encircled the restaurant. Inside, it was cozy with a fire unnecessarily warming the interior. The waiter led them to a small, intimate table, one of only a few in the room.

"They offer a steak here that you would absolutely love," he offered.

As much as she loved a great steak, Laura didn't want him ordering for her, and she wanted something different anyhow. "I would love the Thai Duck Salad with a bowl of soup and a glass of wine," she said to the waitress. Clark seemed disappointed with her order and ordered the steak for himself. Laura noticed the restaurant featured organic produce, local fish, and local wines. Clearly, they served more than just French food.

As if to answer her unasked question, Clark remarked that the original owner featured a mostly French-inspired menu but had sold the restaurant to new owners in early 2000. Still the restaurant served great dinners, and its quaint setting brought in lots of patrons. Their conversation lulled for a few moments and then Laura brought up the subject both knew would surface even during a nice dinner.

"Anything new in your inquiry?" she asked, sipping her wine.

"Nothing new," he said. "The coroner hasn't given us a report yet. He doesn't handle many cases a year and wants to do a thorough job. Her husband said she liked to walk the beach at night and was never afraid, but he always worried something bad might happen."

"Not that it is important, but I thought you might want to know. Mrs. Evans, the housekeeper at the inn, found a scrap of paper in the wastepaper basket of our lodger, with the address of the woman who died scribbled on it. Earlier, when I told him the first name of the woman who had gone missing, he appeared shaken," Laura said.

"Interesting. Check the address he gave when he signed in, and I'll investigate it," he said. Both their salads arrived, and they began eating.

"One thing more," Laura said between bites. "It is probably unimportant but, on the night I arrived, a car was tailgating me after the turnoff at Navarro River. It was late and nobody else was on the road."

"What kind of a car was it?" he asked.

"Just an ordinary kind of an older yellowing white sedan, but it did have a broken headlight to distinguish it," she answered.

"Probably not relevant," he said and smiled broadly at the young waitress who brought their main dishes.

"Maybe not," she replied, wondering why he chose to ignore it. *Why did I bother to tell him anyway?*

They finished their dinner, and he walked her back to her car.

"No more snooping around, young lady," he said. "Just enjoy your stay."

She didn't consider herself snooping. She didn't have a lot to do at the inn. She hadn't even told him about meeting the auto shop owner. She did love a good mystery, however, thinking of her book back at the inn, the one she couldn't seem to appreciate yet. All the way back, she couldn't stop wondering what had happened to Donna.

Seven

"He's no birdwatcher. Nope. He's up to something. Maybe something bad," Mrs. Evans said to Laura as soon as she entered the kitchen the next morning.

Laura ignored her for a moment as she poured herself a cup of steaming hot coffee. She had slept little the night before. Her mind was filled with images of the ocean waves, the lonely beach and the car which had followed her. To make matters worse, the branches of the tall pines near the house rubbed against each other all night, making a moaning sound, and she could even hear a lonely foghorn near the coast. Creaking noises from the settling of the old house added to her uneasiness, and Laura found herself imagining intruders. She was glad it was morning.

"Did you hear what I said?" asked the housekeeper who, Laura noticed, was slurring her words a little.

Has the woman been drinking? Laura thought. "I did hear you, but I am not awake yet. I didn't get much sleep last night," Laura replied out loud.

"Well, I tell you I wouldn't get much sleep myself if I were all alone and staying in this house at night with that man," Mrs. Evans said. "If I were you, I would try to get out before he gets his breakfast."

"What makes you think he isn't a birdwatcher?" asked Laura.

"Besides the fact that he neglects to bring his binoculars with him most of the time, he also makes no effort to explain where he's going and no one in town has seen him much. There doesn't seem to be any reason why he chose this town to visit except for the address he wrote down," she continued.

"I told the sheriff at dinner last night about him. I'm going to look up the address he listed when he registered and give it to Sheriff Clark. He's going to check on our lodger," said Laura.

"You went out to dinner with Jim Clark?" she asked. "Moves fast, doesn't he. Goes out with everyone, he does."

Laura ignored her comments about something so personal. It was none of her business. The housekeeper seemed more interested in hearing Laura had gone to dinner with Clark than getting help on finding information on the lodger.

"Wouldn't be surprised if he was going out with Donna as well. She was going out with somebody, that's for sure," she continued.

"How do you know that?" Laura asked.

"Well," began the housekeeper, who seemed eager to tell her some local gossip. "My best friend's daughter owns the beauty shop in town. You should make an appointment if you need a haircut. She's really good at her job. That gal hears everything and tells her mother, who in turn tells me. It's a small town you know, and everyone knows everyone else's business."

Except what happened to Donna, thought Laura.

"Donna goes in monthly to the shop and she is...was...frank about her flirting. She boasted about her days with the sheriff earlier in her life. She bragged about her looks and how she attracts men... well even women, according to her. I don't know how her husband puts up with it," she said.

"Maybe he didn't," Laura replied.

"Maybe you're right," she answered. "Wouldn't surprise me, really. He was seen and heard a lot lately at the hotel bar getting drunk and complaining loudly about his wife's behavior. She never came in with him, though. Everyone wondered what she was doing while he was drinking at the bar. Not one to stay home knitting, not Donna," she said.

"Well, I'm finished here. The lodger left his door open, but even though I would like to check out his room, I won't. It's not my day to clean anyway. But I was tempted," Mrs. Evans concluded. "I'll be on my way now."

After she left, Laura found herself wondering if the housekeeper checked out her room when Laura left for the day. She was tempted to enter the lodger's room and look around. She knew she shouldn't and had no cause for looking other than her own curiosity.

She battled with herself through a second cup of hot coffee, looking out the front window at the circular driveway and wishing she had asked Evans what time the lodger had left the inn. She lost the battle with herself and strode to the room slowly as if still contemplating her decision, but she knew it had been already decided.

Entering his room, she was struck by its neatness. There were no brochures lying around the room like hers. There were a few maps and the one on the desk had pen marks on it encircling different locations. Without disturbing the map, she looked carefully at the markings and noticed what was circled was Donna's inn at the mouth of the Navarro River, as well as the house above it owned by the owner of the auto body shop in town. Highlighted were some of the narrow roads leading off from Highway One to houses near the village. Nothing was noted north of Mendocino. She found nothing more of interest in the room and hearing his car on the road up to the inn, she carefully shut his door and settled herself in one of the antique chairs in the living room, looking like she was interested in reading her book.

He said nothing to her as he entered the inn, but Laura stood up and said 'Good morning' as the dutiful house sitter she was supposed to be. He only grunted a reply, but she wanted more.

"How was your walk? Any beach walks I should know about?" she said and pointed to the binoculars he remembered to bring.

"Oh.... Yes..." he said. "I think any beach on the coast is interesting."

"Do you take any photos?" she inquired. "I would love to see them."

"Not really. I just like looking. I walk a lot. Tiring, though. Thought I would return early and take a nap. Didn't sleep well last night."

Neither did I, thought Laura. *And you were part of my not sleeping well.*

"I'm going into town. Do you need any new snacks or more wine?" she asked.

"No, thanks." He began walking to his room, not seeming to want to talk any further.

Well, I learned nothing, thought Laura. *I wonder if he does take any photos.* She checked his reservation, copied down the information, and walked out to her car. Maybe the sheriff would learn something useful.

Laura drove into town and visited Clark in his office. She gave him the name, address, and land phone number the lodger used when he signed into the B & B.

"He's probably legit," the sheriff said to Laura. "But maybe this just might set your mind straight."

Clark checked out the name and address first but was stunned when both turned out to be false. It was a real name and address, but the man who answered the land phone was at home and not in Mendocino. He was concerned and surprised when he learned that his name and address were being used falsely. "Do you know anyone who might be using your information?" he asked. But the response revealed nothing. Then the sheriff asked if he knew Donna, but he didn't know her either. Clark assured the worried man that he would call him when he learned something.

"The lodger must have picked out the name from a receipt or on the internet. It's useless trying to find out his identity with the information we have. It is very strange," Clark said, "and I don't like it."

"Well, neither do I, and I'm living there...alone at night!" said Laura.

"Be careful. I'll come and talk with him as soon as I can," he said. "In the meantime, be careful. Don't interact with him unless necessary. Call me at this number if you need me."

He handed Laura his card after he wrote a cell phone number on the back of it.

"It's my personal cell phone number. I don't give it out often," he said.

Laura didn't think that was the case, judging by the remarks of the women at the cheese shop, but she took the card. She thought of Stan's remark that she shouldn't have any reason to call Clark. She wished the couple were coming home sooner than expected. Her friend hadn't even called to check on her house sitting and if she called June, her friend might really worry. Better to wait a while and hope things got better.

Then the sheriff got a call and he didn't look very pleased with the conversation. With each nod of his head and the words he uttered like "oh," "you're certain," and "that changes things."

Laura expected bad news. Clark waited a moment before speaking. He seemed to be gathering his words carefully.

"It was neither a suicide nor an accident," he said. "That was the coroner. Donna was killed before she went into the ocean, or at least she didn't drown. She was struck on the head, but not by a boulder. More likely it was a bat or a large piece of wood because they found splinters in her hair. The coroner is asking for a second opinion elsewhere and will get back to me when he has more information."

Stunned by the new information, Laura struggled for words. "That's too bad and hard for the husband to hear," she said.

"He will be my first suspect," said Clark. "Got to get back to work. Thanks for the information on your lodger. Be careful and lock your doors at night."

"Sure will, Sheriff," she said trying to make light of the matter, but she was frightened nonetheless.

Laura walked back to her car, frowning and upset at the recent news. She opened the door and sat on the front seat for a moment trying to collect her thoughts. As she sat, her cell phone rang, and she recognized the number as that of her soon to be ex-husband. Laura grimaced but took the call. His remarks were short and cold. He wanted to speed up the divorce, saying that he met someone else more suitable, and he would like to get the divorce over as soon as possible.

"Were you having an affair with this woman while we were married? How is she better than me?" she asked and realized she was shouting.

"I knew you would ask that. You are so predictable. Does it matter?" he asked. She could hear the snarl in his voice.

"Well, it shouldn't matter to me anymore," she replied bitterly.

"It is unimportant," he replied. "You must have realized for a long time that we were not compatible. You love old things, and I love new adventures."

"You mean like a new wife," she said.

"I am not getting married right away, if that's what you think," he replied.

"Well, you certainly found someone right away. Were you having an affair?"

Damn him! He always dodges questions he doesn't want to answer.

"Probably some lover from the office," she commented and then she laughed.

"I'm ending this call now," he said. "It doesn't have to be a bitter divorce. You'll find someone suitable for you in the future, I'm sure."

"Maybe I should make myself available on the internet like you did," Laura shouted.

"You will be receiving documents in the mail from my attorney soon. Maybe you should think of getting one yourself." *Did he mean a lawyer or a lover?* Either way his advice was unwanted. Laura ended the call before he did, or at least she hoped she was first.

She thought of going to the cheese shop to assuage her anger but decided to look for something at the jewelry shop of the new woman she had just met instead. She would buy herself a divorce gift, something beautiful she could wear and know she was taking care of herself for once instead of thinking how she could please her husband. The store was located just a block away from the sheriff's office in an old water tower from the village's past. There were many of those old water towers around the town. Some were used as residences, and some were too fragile to use, but this one was occupied by the owner of the jewelry store.

No one seemed to be inside the shop as Laura looked at all the handmade jewelry in the locked cases. Nothing was over fifty dollars, and all were locally designed by artists in the community. She had already decided to buy herself something when Sheila appeared from behind the curtain at the back. Again, Laura was struck by her natural beauty. Her long, smooth raven-colored hair curled just below her chin and her black mascara was deftly applied to show off her dark eyes. She certainly didn't need any jewelry to enhance her features.

"Sorry I didn't hear you. I must get one of those jingling bells like at the wine shop, so I know when someone enters. Can I show you something special?" she asked.

"I want to buy something for myself, and I have always wanted someone to buy me some lapis. Do you have any pieces with lapis in them?"

"Not at these prices, but I do have a few with lapis in them in my back room. Everything you see here is local, but I bought some lapis at a show I attended in Los Angeles. I love the intense blue of lapis as well as you. Let me get the pieces for you," she said and disappeared behind the curtain again. Upon her return, she laid out some jewelry on the counter.

"Do you like any of these?" asked Sheila as she placed the pieces on a square of black velvet to show them off. "So you are buying something for yourself? Going through a divorce?"

"How did you know?" Laura asked.

The woman smiled. "In the jewelry business, we see many things. Men buying women jewelry to impress them, and sometimes a woman buying jewelry for herself. When women buy jewelry for themselves, they either buy it because they can afford it or often as a gift to themselves when they get a divorce."

"Interesting," said Laura. "You're right. I am getting a divorce, and I want to buy myself something to celebrate my freedom. I want to buy something I like, not something he likes."

"Good for you! I recently went through a divorce myself, and this store is my way of doing what I want."

Laura looked at the pieces displayed and loved each of them. One was a ring with the vibrant blue offset by small pearls surrounding the stone and the others were bracelets with smaller lapis stones. All three were more than fifty dollars apiece, but Laura didn't care. *I am going to buy myself something beautiful, and it's going to be the ring.*

"Wow, I do love this ring. How much is it?" Laura asked.

"You have good taste. It is, of course, more expensive than the others, but I could let you have it for five hundred dollars," she said.

Laura told herself it was too much and shook her head. "Sorry," she remarked to the owner. "I shouldn't be spending that much on myself right now."

"I would love for you to have the ring. The best I could do and still make some sort of a profit is...how about four-fifty."

Laura pondered for only a minute and gave in. "I shouldn't, but I'll take it," she said.

The two chatted for a few more minutes about men and divorces. Laura learned that Sheila was indeed interested in the sheriff but was wary. She said they had only dated a few times since she moved to Mendocino. The woman was controlled in her expressions and didn't reveal much as she related both her divorce and her recent attraction to Clark but gave no details. Laura left the jewelry store and walked down the street.

Eight

The woman known as Sheila reflected on Donna's death after Laura left.

Such a beautiful woman. Donna had such beautiful eyes, a sensuous body, one that shouldn't be wasted. But the woman was foolish. She plunged headlong into the unknown with little thought of her safety. Reckless. She didn't even know me, hardly met, and yet the second time we were intimate. She didn't have to say it was her first experience at this, but she was willing to try it all, then more.

Donna seemed headed for trouble, full throttle. Sensing such recklessness, I should have stayed away. But I didn't! The third time we were together, on the beach, she started to show her real wickedness. Her words became vile, uncouth. She had been drinking. Then she started to get mean, really mean. I don't allow that. She should have stopped, but she didn't. Never do I allow filth to be thrown at me like that.

Daddy used to say things like that to me. So did my ex-partner, but I taught them both not to demean me. I have to protect myself. Always will.

Sheila put down the wiring of a necklace she was repairing. Since moving to Mendocino and opening her jewelry store, she was surprised the high prices she could ask for her goods. She thought about the woman who just purchased a ring. *What an innocent. I marked that ring up over one half the cost, and she didn't even flinch.* She laughed to herself, watching the woman leave her store. *Laura would never understand my relationship with Donna.*

Outside, Laura walked away from the jewelry store, fingering her ring lovingly. She wanted to wear it right away even though it was a bit large for her ring finger. She would have it sized back in San Francisco. Buoyed by her purchase, she went to the wine and cheese shop, but nobody she knew was there to appreciate her purchase. Disappointed, Laura bought some bread, cheese, and wine to celebrate by herself back at the inn. Walking by the realty office, she spotted Julie at her desk and walked in.

"Good afternoon," said Julie. "You look very pleased with yourself!"

"I am," said Laura. "I just bought this ring as a divorce present to myself." Laura walked to her new friend's desk and extended her hand.

"It's beautiful. You should go out tonight and wear it to celebrate. By the way, I heard you had dinner with Jim Clark at the hotel."

"Boy, this really is a small town," Laura said. "I don't have any plans for tonight at all, and I really don't want to just sit at the inn with nothing to do."

"If you like, I can get us two tickets to the town play for tonight. The box office is closed, but I know the ticket seller and could call her at home. Want to go?"

Laura didn't hesitate. She did not want to stay at the inn all evening wondering about the solitary lodger. She could worry when she got back. She probably wouldn't sleep that night anyway. "Sounds good. I'll meet you there when it opens."

Laura looked around the room and got an idea when she noticed photos of houses for sale near the inn and ones off Highway One. "You know what you said about staying. Well, I do like it here. Maybe I should look at some houses."

The woman jumped up and grabbed her purse. Even if Laura was just a looker, it gave the realtor a chance to get out of the office. "Let's go," she said. "Boring day sitting behind this desk when the weather is beautiful. We can take a ride around the countryside. What area did you have in mind?"

In the car, Laura asked if there was anything available near the outlet of the Navarro River to the ocean. Also, she asked about property past the Navarro River leading to the town.

"I know an inn that will probably be up for sale soon. Donna's husband will most likely not keep it. He wasn't really interested in the business anyway," she said.

"Maybe just a house will do," said Laura. "I understand the owner of the auto shop lives above that inn."

Julie paused for a moment and looked at Laura squarely. "You have learned a lot about our little town in so short a time."

Laura smiled. "I guess taking care of an inn with a solo guest and not many responsibilities, I have become curious about this mystery."

"Me too," remarked Julie, turning back to her driving. "You know a few of us who stayed in town went to high school together. Some left after high school and never came back. Others left and returned to stay like the sheriff. Did you know he and Donna were high school sweethearts?"

"I heard that. Where does he live?" she asked.

"He rents an old house on the headlands away from the town itself. He came back after his divorce and probably will stay. I hope to sell him something."

"Judging by his success with the women here, he must like his job," Laura remarked.

"He could be the man Donna was seeing," said the realtor. "They were quite an item in the past. Everyone thought they would marry after high school, but they both moved away and married others."

Laura shuddered. *No, not him...well, maybe.* The hair prickled at the back of her neck. *It'll pay to be careful.*

They continued driving toward the Navarro River, when Laura noticed the lane where the driver had turned...on that first night. She wanted to drive down that lane.

"Are there any houses down this street?" she asked.

Julie turned sharply into the lane and stopped the car. "There are a few here, but none for sale that I know of. Doesn't hurt to look and see what style of house you may be interested in."

Each house was different, but similar in that they were wood structures and muted in color to blend in with the countryside. In fact, all of Mendocino exhibited that same grey, weathered look including old barns and broken fences along Highway One. The road narrowed and became difficult to navigate.

"We probably should stop here," said Julie. "There might be some houses up the road, but I have learned since living here not to explore too much. Even though pot has become legal in California, the marijuana growers don't like people trespassing on their property."

"Do you have a map in the car?" asked Laura.

"Here's one," said Julie as she produced one from the driver's side. "What is it you are looking for? We should get back now. You probably want to change before the show."

They drove back to the village without much conversation. Laura wasn't sure whether she should have revealed her curiosity or not. They parted at the realty office and Laura drove back to the inn, apprehensive about meeting up with the lodger. To her delight his car was not there, but as she walked through the living room she spotted his cell phone on the small table on the foyer where June kept a few brochures. He must have forgotten to take it with him when he left.

It was too much for Laura to overlook the opportunity to view its contents. She looked out at the driveway and road again and checked his room, but he was gone. No telling how long. She hurried back to the phone and checked the photos, pleased and surprised to find that his phone was not password protected from intruders such as she. There were no photos associated with bird watching, but a lot of scenes of houses and beaches. She recognized the beach where the Navarro River connected with the ocean. There were several photos showing a woman and a man sitting together on the beach, but the ones taken didn't show the woman's face as she was wearing a hat, and only the back of the man was visible.

Laura placed the cell phone back on the table where she had found it. After being certain she left it exactly the way it had been sitting, she returned to her room and dressed for dinner. *Was the woman in the photo Donna? Who was the man?*

Nine

I never thought this would happen. I didn't mean it to happen. It was an accident. She provoked me. I wouldn't have hit her otherwise. The things she said hurt me. I tried to warn her that I was angry. Why didn't she listen?

The figure cast shadows on the beach as the clouds drifted overhead while walking the length of the same beach where Donna's body had been found. Shuffling in the sand, the figure moved slowly as if to stop time while thinking.

She could be so abusive, so mean, so self- absorbed. Making fun of me, relentless in her remarks, cruel even. I just couldn't take it anymore. Pressure had been building. Why couldn't she have seen that?

There were still large pieces of driftwood lining the beach. Among them was the large piece of wood set adrift in the ocean that was used to kill Donna. It lay among all the other driftwood. It had not been found as yet by the authorities who were searching the area. The figure stopped at the spot where the confrontation had taken place, but the tides had changed the configuration of the kelp and driftwood. Only the sighting of the house in the hills referenced the location.

I wish it hadn't happened. No one saw me. There is no evidence, but I am worried about that woman, Laura, who might just keep snooping around. She worries me.

The inner voice became louder and peace was not possible, so the figure walked back up the pathway worrying more, not less, about a possible strategy, a possible outcome.

How can I keep that woman from nosing around? She has become a real problem and only has added to my anxiety. I don't think anyone will connect me with the information she's gotten so far, but if she keeps looking, she might find the car or worse yet, she might suspect me and look further. I wonder who she has told about her findings? That little group that meets at Mimi's is probably both her source and her sounding board.

Stumbling on a rock while walking uphill seemed to add only more annoyance to the day. There was a couple walking down the path, unusual for tourists on a weekday. Not wanting to be seen, hiding behind a tree was the only way of avoiding them.

I don't like this hiding. Donna had me in the shadows and I didn't like it. Now I realize there were others and I was stupid enough to think she was only seeing me. The woman was a slut. I don't like to think about it, but she didn't deserve to be on this earth.

The couple passed by without even looking near the tree. They were concentrating on the clear, cloudless day and the breathtaking view of the ocean from the path.

When did I stop enjoying seeing Donna? At first, she was charming, fun to be with, exciting even. Little by little she started pushing me. It was small things like when to meet and how often. Then she started using a shriller voice and demanding more attention, more things she wanted to do, more, more, more. It does not seem unreasonable that I finally snapped.

Reaching the road and crossing it was easy, as there were no cars on the highway. Being absorbed in thought was unsafe when crossing the road on the curve where oncoming cars couldn't be seen.

I could easily be run over by a car, but I do want to live. I want this episode to be over, and when it is, I want to change my life and enjoy it more! Maybe Laura should be the one to be in a car accident. That would be a way to solve the problem. I hope it doesn't come to that.

I have got to stop thinking like this. I have enough problems without causing more. And yet, the idea of ridding myself of Laura does sound tempting.

I need to walk some more. I have to continue my everyday activities and act normally among others. I do not want to be discovered.

Ten

The play was an intense drama. Laura had expected an amateur showing but was surprised at the professionalism of the performance. It was comparable to anything she had seen in small theaters in San Francisco. Most of the actors lived in Mendocino and all contributed to the success of the playhouse, including stints at costume design and construction of the sets. It was apparent the small troupe was a tight knit group and worked hard at their craft.

During the intermission, Julie introduced her to some of the actors and others involved in the production. Wines from Anderson Valley were featured along with some organic cheeses and homemade wafers donated by Mimi and Annie. Laura was enjoying the break when they both heard shouting at the other end of the room. Laura spotted Jim Clark arguing loudly with a man she did not recognize. Julie said the man was Donna's husband, Tom Reynolds.

"How do I know it wasn't you who she was seeing?" the man yelled into the sheriff's face.

"Well, it wasn't!" Clark shouted back.

Laura noticed the lady who owned the jewelry store, Sheila, standing next to the sheriff, obviously embarrassed by the confrontation.

"Calm down. You're making a scene. I know you're very upset, but our fighting will not help the situation," remarked the sheriff.

Laura was surprised by how gently Clark was managing the arguing. He seemed to remain calm as the other theatergoers looked on. None of them interfered at first, but then a couple of the men took the husband's shoulders and persuaded him to step back.

"What are you going to do about it?" yelled the man. "Here you are enjoying yourself with yet another woman while my wife is dead!"

The onlookers began mumbling to themselves, and Laura wondered how the sheriff would end this confrontation.

"I'm doing all I can, but right now, as I told you, the case is still being handled by the coroner. Why don't you come to my office first thing in the morning and I can show you all I have," Clark answered.

The husband seemed to have settled down somewhat as the other two men spoke to him softly and led him out of the theater. Just then the lights flashed signaling the resuming of the play, and the theatergoers began returning to their seats. Laura and Julie went inside to join the other playgoers, and she didn't know whether the sheriff returned with his date or not. She didn't know where they were seated.

After the play, Laura and Julie decided to call it a night and Laura walked back to her car alone. She really didn't want to return to the inn, but she knew she must. Walking back down the street in the shadows of the trees, Laura heard the crackling sound of leaves beneath her feet and turned to look behind her. She thought she spotted someone but wasn't certain because the moonlight was playing tricks with the branches of the trees. The evening breeze whistled through the trees. She heard footsteps behind her. *Of course,* she thought, *everyone is leaving the playhouse at the same time and some are going to the hotel for cocktails. That's what I am hearing.*

Still she was nervous and turned her head again to be assured it was just her imagination, but no one was there. Quickening her pace, Laura rummaged through her small purse for the car keys, accidentally spilling its contents on the ground. Swearing to herself, she grabbed it all and jammed the car key into the locked door. Jumping inside she locked her car doors. With a sigh of relief, she put the key into the ignition, grateful she was out of any supposed danger.

She drove quickly out of town, entering Highway One. She raced toward the inn's parking lot. The lodger's car was already there and as Laura passed it, she placed her hand on the hood to see if it was warm. The engine was cold, so she assumed he hadn't been driving his car recently. Relieved that he couldn't have been in town while she was there, she walked more slowly toward the inn's front door and let herself in. Still, she would probably not sleep well.

Eleven

During the night Laura tossed and turned and checked her locked door several times. Finally, she placed a chair against it. She fell asleep and dreamed a lot. The image of someone following her stayed with her in her dream, and its shape took several forms. The first time it was the image of a menacing sheriff following her, his tall lanky body making grotesque silhouettes.

The second dream occurred shortly after the first when Laura returned to bed after getting a drink of water from the bathroom. This time the shadowy figure resembled the lodger who frightened her, and behind him was a third figure who resembled the man arguing with Clark at the theater, Donna's husband, Tom. Laura was grateful for daylight and quickly threw on her robe to get some coffee. It was very early, but the housekeeper was already there.

"Did you get any sleep last night?" Mrs. Evans asked. "I'm surprised you're still here. I would have left!"

"I can't leave until June and her husband return," Laura answered curtly and grabbing a coffee cup, she filled it.

"Well, why don't you call them? They probably would want to know of the events around town," the housekeeper suggested.

Laura left the room without replying but thought it was probably a good idea. She went back to her room for privacy and dialed her friend's cell phone. June answered on the first ring.

"We are coming back early anyway," June said. "We heard the news and want to get back. I'll tell you about our trip later." At the beginning of the last sentence, June lowered her voice and Laura pictured her cupping her hand around the phone for privacy.

"Can you talk?" asked Laura.

"Now I can," said June. "Stan has gone into the gas station office to pay cash as the credit card machine wouldn't work. He is swearing out loud at the inconvenience! He has been in a bad mood the entire trip and the couple where we were staying couldn't help but notice. The wife spoke to me in confidence and asked a lot of questions. I don't know her well and didn't want to tell her much. I need to tell someone. When I get back, maybe we can talk. I think we will sell the bed and breakfast soon. Stan is headed back to the car and I can't talk. He probably threw money on the counter. I need to go. I'll see you soon."

Laura was relieved they were returning. Now she could go home and, even if she had to stay another night, at least there would be others in the house. As she changed quickly into her jeans, the front doorbell rang and Mrs. Evans yelled that she was too busy to answer it. *Who could it be this early in the morning?* Laura wondered.

Outside the beautiful stained-glass window of the front door stood the silhouette of Jim Clark looking like he did in her dream. Laura shuddered at the comparison and opened the door quickly to erase her fear.

"Good morning," he said as he walked past her into the living room. "I wanted to talk with you early before you might leave for the day. I saw you at the theater last night and thought you might have some questions, plus I wanted to check on you as well."

Yes, I do, she thought. *Some questions would be: Do you date everyone in this town? Did you follow me last night? Did you kill*

Donna? Instead she said, "No, I really don't have any questions. Stan and June are coming back early, so I will be leaving soon."

"Well that's a relief…for you, I mean."

Laura just smiled.

"Is your lodger awake? I wanted to ask him some questions too, before he left for the day," he asked.

"It's pretty early still," said Laura and she let Clark follow her as she walked into the kitchen. "Have you seen the lodger?" she asked Mrs. Evans.

"No, and I'm glad of it," she said as she finished up, leaving small plastic tubs for breakfast and snacks. "I am getting out of here as fast as I can."

"I'll just knock on his door," the sheriff said, and Laura followed in his footsteps as he walked down the hall to the room Laura told him the lodger rented. But no one answered his knock. "I noticed his car in the driveway. If he left, he must be walking."

"Do you have a cell phone number for him?" he asked.

Laura thought she had been remiss not to have gotten the number but declined to tell the sheriff she had looked at his cell phone for messages.

"No," Laura said sheepishly.

"I'll leave my card under the door with a message. If either you or the housekeeper see him, please tell him I need to talk to him."

"Did you find out who he is exactly?" asked Laura.

"Not yet," said Clark. "But it's not a crime to register under a false name. I just need to talk with him."

They walked back to the front door and as he was leaving, the sheriff reminded Laura to call him if she needed anything. "Don't be snooping around either. It isn't wise!" he warned and left her with a lot of doubts. After waving goodbye to the housekeeper, she slowly made her way back into her bedroom. Laura didn't want to stay any longer in this house either. Maybe the lodger was in his room and just not answering the door, but his car was still in the driveway. He must have taken a walk. Laura made up her mind and hurried to her car and started driving. But where was she going? Stopping on a shoulder, Laura dialed Julie's number. On the second ring her new friend answered.

"Want to go for another drive?" Laura asked her.

Business was slow at the office and after a promise of lunch at the hotel, Julie gave in and Laura drove to pick her up.

"Where are we going?" she asked.

"I want to go back to that dirt road leading away from Highway One," answered Laura.

"Oh no," said Julie, fumbling with the door lock. "I don't think that is such a good idea."

"There are two of us. I just want to look around," Laura said.

"What are you looking for?" Julie asked.

Laura told her the whole story of how, when she drove into Mendocino that first night on Highway One at the Navarro River, a car had trailed behind her for a few miles, turning off at that same dirt road. She told her the car's description and about the dim headlight. The realtor seemed interested.

"Have you told Jim Clark?" she asked.

"Yes," Laura answered, "But he didn't think it was important."

The other woman hesitated a few moments looking out the window and seeming to think about the idea and its possible consequences. Then she answered. "Okay, I'm in. But maybe you're wrong about the sheriff. And what makes you think it is a man who is involved? Maybe it's a woman. Maybe a wife of someone who Donna was seeing. Did you think of that?"

Laura admitted to herself, *I hadn't thought of that. But it's too late. I want to look down that road myself, for what I really don't know, but the idea of whoever was tailgating me that night is intriguing.*

"No," she admitted to June, "let's go." She started the car without any further questions from either of them and without either further deciding that it was a bad idea.

They left Mendocino heading south on Highway One and turned down the lane. Stopping at the same place as before where the road turned to dirt, they got out of the car. The dust kicked up as they walked, and neither was dressed for a hike.

"Whew, the dust is overwhelming," remarked Julie. "How much farther do you want to go?"

"I see an old barn to the left up away from the lane. Do you see it?" Laura asked.

"Yes," Julie said. "I didn't know it was there. It has to be very old."

"Let's go over there," said Laura. "It isn't far."

"This better be a great lunch at the hotel," remarked Julie. "I'm having a drink as well!"

Before long they reached the old barn. It was weathered, with fallen shingles scattered on the ground, typical of all the old barns dotting the picturesque scenery along Highway One. This one was hidden away unseen. It was a large barn with enormous doors secured only by an ancient latch. No lock.

"We have to go inside," Laura said.

"Or we could just leave and go back to the car," Julie replied.

But her remark was left hanging in the air as Laura undid the rusty latch and pushed open the door by herself. "Someone has been here recently," she said. "It is easy to open and there are marks left on the dirt by opening the door. Can you see them?"

"It looks very dark inside. But I agree that someone has been here recently. Now let's go."

"Just a peek," said Laura. "We've come this far."

They walked slowly into the darkness with Laura leading the way. Neither had thought to bring a flashlight. But just then the clouds outside parted and sunshine threw light onto an old car that was parked on the dirty floor. It was the same old car Laura had seen that first night. She was sure of it.

"Now can we go?" her friend asked.

"Okay," said Laura. "I'm sure it's the same car."

They walked more quickly back to Julie's car and left a trail of dust behind them as they raced back to the highway and people.

"So are you going straight to the sheriff's office?" asked her friend.

Before she could answer, Laura heard the familiar ring of her cell phone and saw it was June calling. "I need to answer this," she said.

"I'm on my way back," Laura told June.

Julie left Laura at the inn. Lunch would be another day. Neither was in the mood anyway. It was decided Laura would return later to the village to retrieve her own car.

Hurrying up to the front door, she saw June standing at the entrance. She looked distraught and ready to talk to a friend. Laura noticed the lodger's car was still there. She guessed he had been out walking all day since Clark had been there that morning.

"So glad to see you," gushed June as she embraced Laura with a hug that left Laura panting for breath. "I hope you don't mind my pouring out my heart to you."

"No, but let's go inside first. Maybe some chamomile tea would help calm you down," said Laura.

"I've been sipping some brandy instead," confessed June.

They sat in the overstuffed chairs in the living room. June sipped brandy while Laura drank her chamomile tea.

"Stan has been in a foul mood ever since we left Mendocino. The couple noticed it, of course, and as I mentioned, we didn't talk much business while we were there. We didn't even go to the wedding. Stan wanted to play golf instead and I thought it might improve his mood, but it didn't. He didn't bring his clubs anyway and had to rent some."

Laura remembered meeting Stan at the house when he had returned to the inn to retrieve his clubs, but she didn't think it wise to bring that up.

"The woman and I talked while Stan was doing other things, and she said although the bed and breakfast business had its ups and downs, they would be staying. But she advised me for the sake of my marriage, maybe it was best to let it go. The only time Stan was least angry was when I said perhaps we should just sell the inn. He relaxed a little after that."

June began sobbing, and Laura went to get some tissue when she noticed the lodger's door had been left open. She quietly pushed the door and looked inside, but he was not there.

Walking back into the living room, Laura heard her cell phone ring and answered it before she met back up with June. The call was from Mendocino. It was Julie.

"I looked up that barn as soon as I got back. Guess who owns it?" she asked, but answered her own question immediately, "Your acquaintance, the creepy owner of the auto shop, owns it."

Laura made a face the realtor couldn't see. "That makes me cringe."

"Me too," said her friend. "I have to go. I'll talk to you later."

Laura ended the call, distressed by the latest news, but decided not to worry June more than she was already. Completely overwhelmed by her own problems, June didn't even ask who called.

"Stan has been such a jerk," June began. "He's always complaining about money problems, not liking to live here, and being tied down to a bed and breakfast. I'm tired of it. I'm going to tell him tonight. I'll call my parents, tell them everything and hope they'll understand. I was hanging on because I didn't want to disappoint them. They don't really like Stan anyway. They don't think we are a good match."

"This whole murder investigation hasn't helped anyone's mood," said Laura. "I didn't tell Stan and I didn't want to upset you, but Julie and I found the old car that followed me that first night. We found it in a barn located right at the end of a dirt road."

"What? Have you been snooping?" asked June. "All we need now is more trouble," she lamented. "What does an old car have to do with anything anyway?"

"Maybe nothing," replied Laura. "But that mechanic guy is really creepy, and it probably belongs to him. He probably doesn't want anyone to know it's there. The barn is located on a road just before this one leading to your inn. It's the same road where the car that was tailgating me the first night turned off Highway One."

"Okay, but still what does that have to do with Donna's death?"

"Well," admitted Laura, "Maybe nothing as I said. But the night I came here, it turns out that was about the time when Donna was killed. It could have been the person responsible. The car was coming from the direction of the beach where the incident occurred," said Laura.

"Why didn't you tell me all this?" asked June.

"I didn't think it was important at the time," answered Laura.

June fell silent, immersed in her thoughts and the revelations she had just heard. Laura thought *I hope she's not mad at me.*

"I should be angry with you for not confiding in me, but I just can't be. I have too much on my mind already. Do be careful, however. I know you have made some friendships here, but it could be dangerous for you," said June.

"You're right, and I apologize for not letting you in on what I've been doing, but I knew you had your own problems," said Laura in her defense.

"Let's keep each other posted," suggested June. "Let's not tell Stan, however. He's got enough on his mind. He would be mad at your involvement, anyway."

"Okay," promised Laura.

When they heard Stan's car in the driveway, June gathered herself together. Laura went to her bedroom to leave the two of them alone. They had a lot to talk about. She began packing as it gave her something to do. After a while June joined her.

"Why are you packing?" she asked.

"You returned, and I should go," Laura answered.

"Oh, please don't go. We could spend some time together. It would be a nice contrast to what is going on here," she said. "I could take you to a winery or two on Highway One twenty-eight in Anderson Valley. There are lots of them strung along beside the road. You should see how beautiful it is in the daylight. Please stay at least for the couple of days you would have been here anyway," June said.

Laura pondered her choices for a moment. She only had a divorce waiting for her in San Francisco and anyway, she had taken the time off from her job. Still curious about the recent events in Mendocino and feeling safer with Stan and June back, Laura decided to stay.

June was elated. "Let's plan on making a day of it tomorrow and I'll have Mrs. Evans make us a basket of goodies to go with a red wine. We will picnic on the grounds of Navarro Winery just like I would suggest to my guests, if we had any. I am going to plan it right now. We can go into the village to shop for what we need."

She left Laura's bedroom without confirming their plans, but that was all right because, Laura thought, *such a pleasant trip would be a welcome relief from the events of the last few days.*

Twelve

Stan looked relieved when Laura and June left the inn in June's car the following morning. They decided he probably needed a respite from them as well. They went to the village for supplies before they left as the housekeeper balked at making lunches for them.

June selected what she wanted and thankfully no one they knew was at the cheese shop to gossip. On the way out, however, a man approached them. June knew him by sight and tugged at Laura's sleeve. "That's Donna's husband, Tom," she said.

He strode directly toward them and surprisingly addressed Laura, not June. "Why are you meddling in my business?" he demanded.

"I didn't think I was," answered Laura. She was guilty as charged though.

"Stay out of it!" he warned and whirling around, walked down the street.

"How did he know about that?" she asked June.

"As well you know...small town," June replied.

They retrieved Laura's car and made their way south on Highway One and turned off at the Navarro River to Highway 128 only to be followed by another car making the journey. Laura didn't express her fear to June but was thankful when the other car proceeded ahead of them as they stopped off at an apple stand.

"I got you a winery map in the village and you can pick one yourself if you want, but I would like to stop at the Navarro Winery for lunch. It has a beautiful view from its picnic tables, and it's my favorite," June said.

"I really like this road and so does my car. I am going to miss driving it," said Laura.

"Do you have to give it up?" June asked. "I love your little black sports car."

"I should. Did I show you my other extravagance?" she asked her friend and crossed her left hand over the steering wheel so June could see her new lapis ring.

"Wow! And you're wearing it on your ring finger," she said. "You really are getting a divorce. Stan used to buy me jewelry. The first two years we were married he was very sweet and attentive. After my parents helped us buy the inn, the problems started. Stan's not handy with tools, so the arrangement was that I would be the one handling the house, the guests, and the help.

"Stan was supposed to handle advertising, publicity, and securing guests and the books. But in the last year he lost interest and hasn't kept up with his part. It showed in our bookings, which were few. Whenever I tried to talk about it, he would only get angry. I think we should sell soon or our marriage will end as well. We still owe money to my parents, but they haven't been pushing it because they know of our situation."

"Sorry. I thought you might have the perfect marriage," said Laura.

"Nobody does. Even my parents admitted they had some rough times. If Stan and I can get through this, I hope we can start again and repair our relationship," she said.

They remained silent for some time, just enjoying the scenery and lost in their separate thoughts. On their way to the wineries on Highway 128, Laura spotted a roadside fruit stand at an apple farm. Anderson Valley had once been home to large sheep and cattle farmers as well as apple orchards that thrived in the lush valley. Over the years, most of these properties were given over to the numerous wineries lining the highway just in Anderson Valley, but some were snugly set back hidden from view. According to June, there were dozens of wineries off the highway, making more to choose from. Most consisted of many acres and featured beautiful grounds as well as buildings.

One of the last holdout apple farms still existed at the beginning of the valley and when Laura saw the sign announcing fresh fruit, she wanted to stop. Her car rested in the dusty parking lot while she looked at her cell phone to note the time. They were not in a hurry, but June clearly was not eager to stop. The idea of stopping at a fruit stand was just too much for Laura to miss, and she persuaded June to stop.

"I won't linger inside," she promised. *Saying this out loud might help me remember to make decisions quickly and not engage in too much conversation.*

But her resolve lessened when a young woman emerged from the back of the open-air building with a smile and welcoming demeanor. June seemed to relax, and Laura noticed June browsing through the fresh fruit section deciding what to buy and moving on to the shelving on the back wall with preserved jams and jellies.

Laura listened politely at the young woman's sales talk about the family farm that had been operating the orchard for generations. *The woman really isn't selling apples, but the concept of a small, established farm still producing products from the love of the land. I do wonder if she really wants this life, but her enthusiasm seems genuine.*

Laura bit into the small apple the woman offered as a sample. As she crushed the apple in her mouth, a sweet yet sour taste filled her taste buds. It was delicious. As the young girl kept describing the varieties of apple her family grew on the farm which lay behind them, Laura picked up a big bag of dried, sliced apples, as well as a pound of the fresh green apples she had tasted.

The young girl waved goodbye as June and Laura returned to their car. Laura placed her purchases on the back seat beside the picnic lunch. *I wish we had more time to spend wandering around the farm with the old apple trees and the newly planted ones,* she thought. As she pulled out, Laura noticed a small wooden structure, which she assumed housed toilets. There was a sign indicating one was for men and one was for women with a drinking fountain in front. For some silly reason, she thought, this structure only adds to the authenticity of the scene.

Laura finished nibbling on her apple as she drove with one hand on the wheel. Highway 128 had become flatter, she noticed, as she entered more of Anderson Valley and signs for wineries began to appear. First, they stopped at a winery June thought Laura might enjoy if only for its beautiful architecture. The building had been designed by an associate of Frank Lloyd Wright and its modern edges framed part of the beautiful valley below. In the tasting room, June specifically asked for a wine whose label featured an elaborate silk-screened drawing of a dragon entwined around the outside of the bottle itself.

They sampled various wines, and Laura bought a bottle for which the winery had won a gold medal. June bought a case. Laura also bought a bottle with the elaborate dragon design because of its beauty.

"We could picnic here," remarked Laura as she surveyed the picnic tables dotting the hill up toward their car.

"Another day," June answered.

Then they drove to the Navarro Winery on the road for their picnic lunch. June bought a half case of her favorite gold medal pinot noir after they sampled yet more wine. They opened a bottle of pinot noir on a picnic table overlooking the property. June had brought along some snacks in a wicker picnic basket and she spread them on the table to Laura's delight. She loved picnics and her soon to be ex-husband didn't like them at all. He wasn't into sitting on the ground while eating!

"You thought of everything," Laura gushed. "This pasta salad you bought at the cheese shop is exceptional. What's in it?"

"Besides the ziti, it has sweet caramelized onions, crumbled goat cheese, and sautéed mushrooms. They put parsley on the top and sometimes large crunchy brown croutons. But I don't see any croutons today," she said as she forked through her Styrofoam cup.

"It's delicious. And it goes well with this pinot noir you chose."

"I have done a lot of reading on wine and cheese pairings. I needed information for the inn. Brie goes well with pinot noir, but you mentioned you already tried that combination. Have some slices of apple we bought at the apple farm," she said as she used a paring knife to slice a green apple. "You certainly have made a lot of friends at the cheese shop."

"I went there most days. I met Julie and the new owner of the jewelry shop where I bought my ring. She is very beautiful," said Laura.

"Stan noticed her right away, too. I hear she's dating Jim Clark, but he'd better watch out. She has quite a temper."

"How do you know that?" Laura asked.

"Your friend Julie was passing by her store one day when she heard her arguing on the phone with someone. Her door was open, and Julie heard her all the way to the street. She was screaming about something."

"Maybe it was her ex-husband," said Laura.

June looked at her friend quizzically and said, "She doesn't have an ex-husband. She's not as talkative as the other women at the cheese shop, but she let it be known she was getting away from her ex-lover by moving here."

Laura wondered why the woman had lied to her, but then she was selling her a ring and wanted to align herself with the customer. It wasn't much of a lie.

"Did she tell you that her ex-lover has a restraining order on her?" June asked.

"No," said Laura aghast. "I guess I just took her at face value. How did you find that out?"

"The sheriff told Roberta's husband, who told her," said June. "Of course Clark should have never told him, but personal matters and professional matters get blurred in a small town. Apparently she was drinking too much on a date and revealed it to the sheriff. She said her ex-boyfriend was going out with another woman. She flew into a rage and followed him to the other woman's house and banged into his car. She had to pay damages, and he put a restraining order on her."

"That's understandable," said Laura.

"But wait," said June gleefully as she leaned forward. "That's not the best part. She shouldn't have told Clark all this after a couple of glasses of wine. She must have forgotten for a moment that she was relating all of this to a law enforcement officer. He got curious and investigated. Turns out the person whose car she banged up was a woman and not a man," said June.

"Oh," said Laura. "That does put a different slant on the situation. Why would she lie to the sheriff?"

"You would have to ask her," said June.

"Don't think I will," replied Laura. *The women in this village have already warned me not to take things at face value*, she thought.

"Have you talked with Stan about all this?" asked Laura.

"Stan doesn't like Jim Clark, so I don't bring him up in conversation much. Stan is livid that he came around the inn while he was gone."

"I'm sorry. I didn't know that," said Laura.

"It's all right," said June. "He will get over it." She began putting the glassware and leftovers in the basket. Laura would have liked another glass of wine and more conversation, but it was evident June needed to return to the B & B.

They walked back up to Laura's car and nothing more was said about the sad situation until they returned to the village to get June's car, and both drove back to the inn. They found Clark waiting on the porch while Stan was inside the house trying to look like he was busy. Looking slightly awkward, the sheriff approached June right away as she entered the house with Laura.

"I hear from Stan your lodger is still missing," Clark said.

"I wouldn't say missing exactly. He has paid for the month and perhaps he decided to stay somewhere else for a time," June remarked.

"Your housekeeper found a slip of paper with Donna's address on it in his waste basket. That's why I am asking."

Stan emerged from the house, having heard the last comments. His face showed anger as he asked Laura a question. "Why didn't you tell us about this?" asked Stan. Laura just looked away from his angry glare.

"I ...well...we just were talking about other things," she answered lamely.

Stan grunted and left to return into the house.

The sheriff continued questioning both women. "Is there anything else you should have told me?"

Laura thought maybe she should tell him about finding the car in the barn owned by Larry of the auto shop. But she was embarrassed as she hadn't told June yet, and maybe this second omission of information would hurt their friendship. After all, Laura should be driving home then.

Clark asked the obvious question. "Why are you still here, Laura? I thought you said you would be returning to San Francisco when Stan and June returned."

As if to save her friend embarrassment, June answered for her. "Laura took time off work and I thought maybe she could finish off the week as planned, and we could spend some time together."

"Oh," said Clark. "Well, I warn you to be careful, especially with the lodger missing. One more thing I must tell you. We found a dead branch we think was used to kill Donna. There are little bits of hair embedded in it. There was also a crumpled note with a time indicated on it: eight-thirty pm. The teenagers found it on the beach just recently. Donna was supposed to meet someone there. I don't know if you knew about that. It's important because that was about the time she was killed. We may be able to connect the writing on the note with someone, but since it was printed, it's a long shot."

As he left, the screen door banged behind him, and Laura and June watched as he walked down the steps. He turned around at the bottom and added, "I talked with the teenagers who hang out at the Navarro River beach when they should be in school. They said the night of the incident they spotted Donna and a man down at the beach away from them. They recognized her, but he had his back turned to them. They also said a woman appeared the next day and quizzed one of the girls about the incident. She didn't give them her name, and the description would fit a lot of people including you, Laura." He turned back to his car without saying anything else. Laura decided not to tell him it was she the teenagers were referring to. Laura thought he already suspected her anyway.

"I could use another glass of wine," Laura remarked, and June quickly brought them both a second glass of pinot noir, which they sipped sitting on the wicker chairs as they watched the sun lower into the horizon.

"That's what happens when you get away for a while. You have to come back to all your problems," said June.

"Aside from the tragedy, Mendocino is a beautiful place to visit," answered Laura.

Just then Stan appeared on the porch. He still seemed angry, but then Laura had not seen him any other way.

"I told Laura she shouldn't ask for his help, and I don't like him visiting us all the time. It's my turn to take a ride. I won't be back for dinner, so you two can go into town if you want," he said, and walked to his car in the driveway.

"Is he ever not angry?" asked Laura.

"Just when I say maybe we should sell this place. I might talk to Julie about it soon," remarked June, who headed back into the house.

They decided to take Stan's suggestion and drive to the village for dinner. On the way they changed their minds and went to a restaurant June suggested on the banks of Little River. Laura was pleased with her idea. The sprawling grounds and multi-story main house enchanted her. They parked their car at the bottom of the hill in the parking lot and walked up to the immense gingerbread-style house with white awnings and cutout shutters. The view as they walked up the hill climaxed at the grand doorway. When the two entered, a young woman asked if they had reservations. June replied she knew the owners and perhaps didn't need a reservation if there was room. The hostess seated them at a table with a white linen tablecloth, a rose scented candle in the middle, encircled with flowers from their gardens.

"This setting is lovely," said Laura as she looked around.

"Stan and I came here often in the beginning. I wonder what secrets this room holds. Maybe Donna and her lover came here, but then everyone in town would know," said June.

"You're right about that. It seems keeping a secret in this village is difficult, but Donna managed somehow. The women I met at the cheese shop had their suspicions but didn't know the man's identity for certain," Laura answered.

"Maybe it was one of the women who didn't like Donna. She was a big flirt. We went out with them a couple of times when we first moved here, but I really didn't want to continue the relationship. Her husband seemed upset by her flirting but said nothing while we were out with them. What he said to her when they returned home I don't know. The other women who are B & B owners didn't like her at all, for the same reason. The town gossiped about their angry confrontations when they thought no one was looking. They had one when they returned to the parking lot after one of our meetings."

"Do you think her husband is a prime suspect?" asked Laura.

"Stan does, and so does the sheriff, I assume, after what happened at the hotel the other night," she replied.

"What happened?" asked Laura.

"We bed and breakfast inn owners hold our semi-annual, casual dinner meeting at the hotel to discuss advertising ideas, business costs, ways of attracting new tourists, and communication ideas. There were about six or seven couples at the meeting.

"We were seated at two large round tables made up specifically for us that night in the larger downstairs dining room. Stan and I were not seated at Donna's table, but we could hear her and see her swinging her hair about, laughing loudly at jokes, and generally playing up to the other husbands. She was wearing a dress with a low-cut bodice with slit sides. I saw her resettling the lower part of her dress often to show off her legs.

"I noticed Donna's husband, Tom, was silent and drinking a lot and my friend who was seated at the next table said she saw him have at least three strong drinks and eat very little of the food he was served. It was the same with Donna. My friend said Donna seemed bored by the business discussion at the table and just wanted to engage in small talk.

"After dinner, some of us lingered outside the hotel just finishing off our conversations when we heard Donna and her husband go at it. They were screaming at each other and finally Donna drove off angry. It was quite a scene. I think he has a strong motive, from what I hear about their marriage."

"What about Larry, the auto shop owner, who lives above their house? Would he do something like that?"

"Larry adored Donna, and she just taunted him. The people in town who have known him since high school say he was always odd...a loner with few friends. Never dated, never went to any of the social activities like most teenagers, and never even went to the beach parties below his parents' house. If Donna and her lover met often at the beach below him, he must have seen the two of them sometimes. The teenagers say they often spot him looking at them through his telescope. Sometimes the light reflects down at them. The teenagers like to taunt him sometimes, but he has never really bothered them."

"Did I tell you I met him at his shop in town?" Laura remarked.

"No, did your car break down?" she asked.

"No." Laura blushed. "I faked a needed car repair and went into his shop. I wanted to see what he was like."

"You really got involved in this, didn't you?" said June.

"I love a good mystery, and this is a real one," she said, thinking of the book she hadn't been reading since she arrived. "Jim Clark thinks I'm just being nosy."

"He might have a good point there and besides, this is real and someone out there is dangerous. You should stay out of it."

Laura said no more on the subject and didn't tell June about going with Julie to the barn where they discovered the car that had followed her that first night.

Probably not a wise move, she thought.

The two enjoyed the rest of the meal without any more discussion about Donna. On the ride back to the village, June confessed she had made plans with someone the following afternoon before all this happened and apologized ahead of time for her absence. Laura was inwardly glad because she wanted to talk with Julie again and perhaps persuade her to return to the barn for a more extensive look. She retrieved her car from in front of the realty office but decided she would wait until the next day to talk with Julie again.

Thirteen

June left before noon the following day as her destination was a couple of hours' drive away from where they had stayed previously. Laura was left alone with Stan at the inn as the lodger hadn't returned. If Stan weren't there, she might have given the lodger's room another look, but he hung around the house without much conversation between them. After all, their only link was Laura, and she couldn't think of any other topics they could discuss. The housekeeper left after breakfast, still grumbling about the lack of guests, and Stan paced around the rooms catching Laura trying to read the book she had brought with her.

"I hope Clark doesn't return again today. You know, he was probably the one who was seeing Donna," he said.

Laura didn't really want any confrontation with June's husband, so she just said, "Maybe so."

"I don't think there is any single woman or married one who hasn't gone out with him," he added.

"Well, he is good looking," Laura remarked, not keeping her resolve of not taunting him. Since she couldn't talk and read at the same time, she placed the book marker and closed her book.

"I guess you could say that," he relented and walked away.

Surprised at his lack of any further responses, Laura decided it was time to leave.

"Think I'll go into the village now," she called after him. Grabbing her jacket and purse from her bedroom, she headed out to her sports car. At the very least, she would enjoy the drive and maybe pick up some news in town.

Laura decided to do a little snooping and check out where the sheriff lived. She parked her car on Main Street in front of the hotel. Facing the ocean on the bluffs was a set of old wooden cottages from another era. Cloistered together at the top of the headlands with only two narrow streets separating them, they were like lone vestiges of a distant past. Laura had walked the few blocks, taking with her only a cell phone and wallet. She took some photos of the houses as they were picturesque and quaint. She didn't know which one belonged to Jim Clark. Then she heard someone call her name.

"Laura, are you interested in becoming my neighbor?" said the sheriff, smiling at her from the front porch of one of the houses.

How embarrassing, thought Laura. *He caught me. What do I say now?*

"Maybe," she said. "Julie said this was an interesting part of town, but no one was selling right now."

"Would you like to see what one looks like inside?" he asked.

Laura hesitated for a moment before answering. "Sure. How come you're home?" she asked.

"Taking a break for lunch. You could share some with me if you want," he replied.

"I'll take you up on your invitation to peek inside, but I'm meeting Julie in town for lunch," she lied, deciding he should know someone knew where she was at the moment.

"It's perfectly safe," he assured her. "After all, I am the sheriff."

He gestured for her to enter, and when Laura did, she was

amazed how modern and updated the interior of the house was compared to the ramshackle appearance of the exterior.

"Wow, you would never expect the renovation of the inside of these cottages. Are all of them updated inside like this one?"

"Yes," he said. "I'm just renting. I wouldn't be able to afford to buy one on my salary, but I do love living here. Make yourself comfortable." He gestured that she should sit on the sofa, but Laura said she needed to leave.

"Meeting Julie for lunch, as I said." She walked back toward the door.

"Then maybe another time," he replied. "Are you sure you weren't just checking up on me?"

Laura didn't respond but walked back toward Main Street, turning to wave at Clark who was still on the front porch, smiling. *How embarrassing*, she thought. As she approached the hotel, she called Julie.

"I'm in town. I still owe you that lunch. Interested in taking me up on my offer?" she asked.

"Might as well," said Julie. "Business is really slow and I need an excuse to get out. Meet you at the hotel in thirty minutes."

"I'll see you there," said Laura

It was a weekday and there were very few tourists in town. She decided to visit Annie's organic grocery store while she waited for Julie to be free. It was located on a side street in an old church building. Entering the anteroom that served as the receptacle for hundreds of brochures on an old battered wooden table, Laura found herself in a cluttered large oblong room with dozens of fresh organic vegetables strewn on long tables. On the left side of the room were two refrigerators featuring some meats but mostly different kinds of milk, juices, and other refrigerated items. The back wall held some household items and the facing wall was dominated by wide, wooden stairs leading up to what had presumably been the choir loft. The second story balcony held jars and jars of dried herbs, carefully labeled with their names but not for their usage. Also on the second floor were various candles and teas.

The entire building gave off an earthy aroma and a nostalgic glimpse of the 60s hippie era. *I love this,* thought Laura. *I have to buy something.* She chose some tea from the second floor and a candle. Then she spotted Annie at the cash register as she walked down the staircase.

"Annie," she said. "I love your store."

Annie looked up and smiled at her new friend. Wearing yet another long-sleeved cotton dress that fell to her ankles, she walked out from behind the cash register to acknowledge Laura.

"How are you?" Annie asked.

"I've been better," said Laura truthfully. "Have you any herbal tea that would help?" she asked, showing Annie what she had selected.

"Oh, I've got a better one for you than what you picked out," Annie said and walked off toward the stairs to get a different tea. Laura was left to wait at the cash register.

Just then a teenage girl entered the store and Laura recognized her as the one she had spoken with on the beach. The young girl headed right to the refrigerator and opened it, getting a cold juice from inside.

"Do you remember me?" Laura asked the girl.

The teenager turned around, looking to see if Laura was addressing her. She looked at Laura squarely but didn't display any recognition.

"I met you on the beach the other day... the beach where they found Donna's body," said Laura.

"Yes, I do remember," said the girl. "We know now it was not an accident."

"Apparently not," Laura replied.

"That creep, Larry, has been hassling us more ever since. You know the guy who lives above the beach on the hill, the guy who owns the body shop in town. He won't leave us alone. Keeps asking us if we saw anything," she related. "He is beginning to frighten us. He was just odd before, and we teased him. No more. We have started going to a different beach... not as good, but we feel safer there."

"Did you tell the sheriff?" asked Laura.

"No," said the girl, twisting off the cap of her juice. "He wouldn't do anything anyway. They know each other. Fat chance he would tell Larry what to do. He's probably scared of him too. See ya." She skittered out the door without paying. Annie came down the stairs with the loose tea she had chosen for Laura and saw the teenager leave.

"Do you know each other?" asked Annie.

"I met her on the beach where they found Donna's body," said Laura. "She said Larry has really been bothering them lately. They have stopped going there."

"We all thought he was harmless," said Annie. "But after what has happened, we aren't so sure anymore. Odd duck, that one, and we have some really odd ducks around here. There has been much talk lately about how he mooned over Donna. She wouldn't slow up on her teasing and taunting him."

"She didn't pay, by the way," Laura said.

"Who didn't pay?" Annie asked.

"The girl didn't pay for her juice," Laura said.

"Oh, I thought you meant Donna. No, that girl comes in every day after school and pays me once a month."

"Well," said Laura. "I'm meeting Julie at the hotel for lunch. I had better start walking over there. Thanks for the tea," she said and paid Annie at the register for her purchases. Laura headed to the hotel where Julie should be waiting.

Entering through the stained-glass doors into the musty interior, Laura was again taken back into a different era. She wondered what stories the hotel could reveal if the walls could talk. There must have been bar fights and jealous husbands back in the times that would make great reading. *But there is intrigue today as well*, she thought, as she spotted her friend.

Laura headed to the bar with Julie following behind her. "It's early for wine, but who cares?" remarked Laura as she ordered two glasses of chardonnay.

"Will you be having lunch with us as well?" asked the bartender.

"Yes," laughed Laura, "we also ordered some sandwiches, but for now we're going to sit in the parlor in those wonderful overstuffed chairs and drink our wine." She pointed to the lobby.

"You were certainly glad to get out of the office," said Laura. "You must have left shortly after I called."

They brought their glasses of wine with them as they sat in the main room of the hotel.

Julie sipped at her wine and indicated she wasn't returning to the office. "Not even planning on going back," she offered. "And I am treating myself to an early afternoon liquid refreshment. I deserve it!"

"June said she and Stan might be selling soon, and I encouraged her to hire you as their realtor."

"Too bad the inn didn't work out for them, but there is a lot of competition, and not everyone realizes how much work it takes to make a success out of that business. Some people buy an inn thinking they can just enjoy themselves like they were guests. But when you own the place, it is a different story. It's like living in a gilded cage that you manage, keep up, and still smile when the plumbing breaks down. You have to be a solid couple to be successful," she said. "Maybe selling is the best idea to save their marriage."

Laura didn't want to ruin their nice lunch, but she had an ulterior motive she needed to reveal. As they were served sandwiches, she brought up the idea.

"Are you up for going back to the barn to take a second look?" she asked timidly.

"I knew you were going to bring it up and I should say *no*, but you've made me curious as well, especially after I discovered Larry owned the property. I didn't know he owned anything but his parents' old home."

"Let's go," urged Laura and both gulped down their last bits of wine and sandwiches. "We can take my car."

"That's part of the adventure," said Julie, following her to the entrance and out the door.

The drive was easy, and they turned off at the road where they had first gone. They stopped when it became too difficult and dusty for Laura's car, and walked to the barn.

"There used to be a house here." Julie pointed out the remnants of a foundation near the barn. "According to the records, Larry only bought the property recently...a couple of years ago. What he wants it for I haven't a clue, but it looks like he is storing at least one car here."

"Maybe he's going to fix up old cars, but the car we saw was not rare or particularly valuable. It is curious. Why would he keep it here?" asked Laura.

"I don't know," replied Julie, "but let's check it out."

They opened the large, decaying barn door more easily this time and when they entered the barn, it was empty.

"That's a surprise," remarked Julie.

"Since we're here, let's look around," said Laura. They each took a part of the barn, but what they were searching for, they didn't know. The barn contained little but old, moldy straw and rusted iron machinery parts. There was little of interest now that the car was missing. They both jumped back in fright when they heard a car driving up the lane, throwing dirt and rocks as it came down the road. In all the blowing dust and dirt from the car coming down the road, both of them were unable to determine the make of the car or the driver's identity.

"We can't leave now. Whoever it is will see your sports car. I'll just use my realtor's status as an excuse. It really isn't a very good one, as we shouldn't have gone inside without permission."

"I don't recognize it, but it doesn't look like the car that was stored inside the barn," said Laura.

The vehicle stopped short of the barn, and when the door opened, they recognized Larry as the driver. He didn't look happy about their being on his property.

"What are you doing here?" he asked.

Julie answered with her realty excuse, but Larry didn't look as if he was buying it.

"So, your little sports car works just fine," he remarked, staring at Laura. "Was your husband pleased there was nothing wrong with it? Does he want to move to Mendocino?"

Julie looked at Laura with inquiring eyes but said nothing about the myth of a husband staying with her in Mendocino.

"He likes it, and I was wondering what this little lane had in the way of houses."

"But why do you need a barn? I thought your husband wasn't handy."

Laura searched for an excuse. She was getting very good at lying. She had to think of something quickly.

"It turns out the wood shingles from these old barns are very valuable, and I've been intrigued by all the weathered barns scattered along Highway One since I came here. Just wondered what they looked like inside," said Laura.

Julie looked relieved by her quick comments, but both wondered if he believed them.

"Really? Well, you both are trespassing."

Laura really wanted to leave, but Larry was blocking her from going toward her car. He was bigger than she remembered and much bulkier. He was standing straight up like a bear does when it's angry and he had placed his hands on his hips, expanding his size outwards. His menacing look with his raised eyebrows and tightened lips only added to her fears. Laura was terrified, and the idea he may have been the person who killed Donna didn't help. He wasn't just a quirky, odd man in the village anymore; he was a real threat to them both. She had to gather up her courage.

"Julie has to get back to the office now. She told the others where we were headed. They will worry if we don't return soon," Laura lied. Julie nodded her agreement.

"We're leaving now," she asserted bravely, walking toward him.

Surprisingly, he waved them both to walk past him to Laura's car. "No one is keeping you here."

They returned to the car, and Laura opened it with her remote control. They both slid inside. As she started the ignition, Laura rolled down her car window and yelled to Larry. He hadn't moved and was still standing with his hands on his hips, staring after them. "Thanks for the peek, Larry!"

They both sighed heavily as Laura headed back to Highway One on the narrow dirt road.

"Whew! That was really frightening," said Julie. "He is very intimidating."

"Do you think he could have been the one who killed Donna?" asked Laura.

"He has no friends and if Donna, whom he admired, mocked him on the beach. He might have exploded."

"That's a thought. Should I tell the sheriff?" asked Laura.

"Only if you want him to lecture you again," answered Julie.

They drove back to town in silence, processing their encounter with Larry. Laura left Julie at her office. They both mentioned calling each other, but not until the next day.

Fourteen

As Laura drove up to the inn, she noticed June's car was still absent and she dreaded being back with only Stan for company. As she entered the inn, she found him sitting in the living room, drinking beer. Two empty cans were on the coffee table in front of him. She hoped just to pass by him without comment, but he looked up from the magazine he was reading and spoke in a mocking tone. "Did you see our sheriff while you were in town?"

Laura just kept walking to her room, but ignoring him didn't work. He spoke again. "Maybe it was her husband instead of the sheriff who killed her. He is the jealous type."

"Maybe," responded Laura. She couldn't be totally rude to the man whose house she was living in. Shutting the door behind her, Laura hoped June would not be too much longer in returning. But she couldn't be sure when June would return, and having nothing to occupy her mind in the meantime, she decided to lay out the possibilities. Was it Larry, the sheriff, or the husband who killed

Donna? Could it be the lodger? Could it be a woman who didn't like her flirting? The last idea didn't seem probable, but possible.

An hour went by, and Laura became tired of doodling the possibilities on paper and went back into the living room. Stan was on his cell phone talking with June. She could hear him trying to calm June down. Apparently, the car wouldn't start, and she was going to call someone for help. Laura waited until he finished the call before she volunteered to pick up June, a few hours away. She needed an excuse to get away from the inn and Stan thought it was a good idea so he agreed. The drive would be a great distraction.

She started down Highway One south and when she passed the lane where she and Julie had discovered the barn, a car turned out from the lane and trailed behind her. In the afternoon daylight, Laura couldn't be certain it was the same older, white sedan that followed her that first night. Her imagination began working overtime, however, and Laura convinced herself it was the same car.

Was it her imagination or did the car seem to be closing in on her back bumper? Laura sped up in response to her fear, but the car behind her followed suit. Soon they were embraced in a common speed, which was excessive for this twisting, narrow road. Laura's cell phone was just beside her, but she feared grabbing it would mean losing focus on her driving, and staying on the road was a key priority. Who would she call? Stan? Julie? The sheriff? She wished somebody could help her right now, and even if it would be dangerous to have another car on the road, it would be a relief if somebody knew of her danger.

Just then the car trailing her lurched ahead and bumped her rear fender on the left, pushing her sideways off the road, forcing her toward the cliff's unprotected edge. Fear crept quickly into her psyche as she envisioned herself plunging into the ocean. Mercifully, a large boulder blocked such a fate, and Laura crashed into it. The other car sped away, leaving Laura to fend for herself.

Blood was streaming down her face from her head smashing into the steering wheel. Looking around, Laura didn't see her cell phone, which had fallen in the crash. She struggled out of the car and screamed down the cliff at the teenagers below on the beach. The stronger ones climbed up the hill while someone else on the beach called 911. Only a few minutes later, she heard sirens approaching.

"We called for an ambulance," said one boy.

"Did you see the car that bumped into me?" she asked the teenagers with her forehead bleeding and throbbing under the sweater they had given her to use as a compress.

"Not really," he said. "We heard a crash and looked up and saw your car up against the boulder. Sorry, I didn't see anyone else."

The sheriff didn't arrive until after she had already been put into the ambulance. "Catch us at the hospital, Sheriff!" the driver shouted, and turning off the siren, drove off. They transported Laura to the local hospital north of Mendocino in Fort Bragg.

Laura was still struggling, her head in pain. She was shaken from the crash and the emergency staff did not want her to sleep. She heard the voices of a man and a woman. She opened her eyes and saw Julie looking concerned and the sheriff looking angry.

"I thought I told you to stay out of this!" he snarled.

"I was just going to pick up June," Laura replied, in her somewhat dizzy state trying to tell her version of the accident.

"You needn't explain. Julie told me all about the barn you found," he said. "And your snooping."

Julie looked away from Laura, and she was left to answer his angry stares.

"I just was curious. We didn't mean any harm," remarked Laura in her own defense. And, she thought, *Where were you when this happened? Were you the one behind me?*

"Well! Did you see who it was that hit you?" he asked.

"No, I was too busy trying to survive."

"Was it the same car you spotted before?"

"I think so," she answered.

"You think so," he mimicked. "That's hardly conclusive. The kids on the beach didn't see another car, but if there was one, someone is trying to warn you, or possibly kill you, to get you to back off. You had better take this seriously."

"What do you mean *if* there was one?"

He ignored her question. "The highway patrol will find out if there was a car that intentionally bumped into you, but it will take time for them to investigate. In the meantime, stay out of trouble."

"I can't go anywhere," she said. "The doctor said I suffered a concussion and need to stay here. I can't drive back to San Francisco for a few days anyway. My car isn't damaged much, and of all things, they towed it to Larry's auto shop!"

"That's unfortunate," Clark said, and slammed out of the room without saying anything else. Laura was relieved to have only Julie in the room.

"He certainly seems mad at you!" Julie said. "He could have been a little more sympathetic, given your condition."

"Have you considered it might have been him following me?"

Julie looked dismayed. "No, I really hadn't considered that. I wish this business was over," she said.

"So do I," replied Laura and she laid back on her pillow and relaxed a little, knowing she was safer in the hospital than anywhere else.

<h1 style="text-align:center">Fifteen</h1>

Laura was released the next day. By then June had returned to Mendocino and drove up north to Fort Bragg to be at Laura's side in the hospital. Both June and Julie wanted her to return to San Francisco, but since the doctor advised against driving, Laura had to stay. She didn't feel safe anywhere in Mendocino, and she just wanted to go home.

Sheriff Clark advised her to check in at the hotel where he could keep an eye on her. Since Laura thought it was a possibility that it could be the sheriff who killed Donna, she chose to stay back at the inn farther away from his presence. Stan was more hospitable when she returned and, since the solitary lodger was still missing, she was relieved. Julie had arrived to check on Laura, and all three women sipped an afternoon tea on the front porch together and worried out loud.

"Such events have never occurred in our small village before," remarked Julie. "Certainly, we have our share of felonies, but most are linked to people on drugs or those that choose to live on the fringe of the county itself. Nothing like this has ever happened in the village. The locals are really upset about it and are trying to keep it to themselves rather than discourage tourists."

"Even the *Mendo Beacon* has mellowed its coverage, hoping the crime will be solved soon. That's why they didn't report this incident. It might have been road rage or an accident. Until it has been declared something else, they don't want to alarm people. But the local gossip has been running full force, and everyone has their suspicions," said June. "Stan still thinks the sheriff is involved."

On cue, Clark appeared, turning down the lane toward the inn. The women were silent in their thoughts as he drove up, knowing he probably brought bad news with him.

"Good afternoon, ladies," he said as if it were a social visit. "Sorry I was so rough with you at the hospital, Laura. I was upset you were involved in an automobile accident."

"It was no accident, Sheriff," Laura said coldly. "It was intentional."

"That isn't why I came to see you. I wanted all of you, including Stan, to know I have arrested someone."

"Who?" asked Laura.

"Donna's husband, Tom," Clark replied. "We heard from their friends and neighbors they have been quarreling a lot lately and Donna told several people she was going to get a divorce. But of course that is not enough for a warrant. What clinched it were several notes we found at her place written by her that seemed to implicate her husband. I can't tell you the exact contents, but together with the teenagers on the beach that witnessed him striking her before, it was enough to arrest him. We are continuing to collect information."

"What about the lodger? He could be implicated," said Laura.

"He hasn't committed any crime that we know of yet."

"Seems like a premature arrest," Laura mumbled under her breath so the sheriff could not hear.

"What did you say?" he asked.

"Nothing important," replied Laura. "Did the Highway Patrol support my being intentionally hit by another car?"

"Not yet," said the sheriff. "But they're looking into it."

"I have to continue on with my investigation. I am going to talk with Larry about the abandoned barn you told me about and the car as well. Don't go to the barn again," he warned. He turned and walked back down the steps to his car and waved goodbye with his hat as he entered the driver's side.

"Such a ladies' man," said Stan in a disgusted tone showing up on the front porch. "Too much nosing around," he said and slammed the screen door on his way back into the house.

The three stayed on the porch until sunset when the sun sank slowly into the horizon, leaving a faint glow behind on the ocean. Reluctantly they went inside and Julie drove home. June, Stan, and Laura ate snacks Mrs. Evans had laid out for them and spoke little. Laura went to her bedroom early, feeling safer than before but looking forward to driving back to San Francisco in a few days. The doctor at the hospital had given her some sleeping medication, which she gratefully took for some much-needed rest, but they also caused her to dream.

Her subconscious played out the scenario of the car wreck, but this time Laura plunged into the ocean silently. She tried to scream but couldn't. She awakened instead in the middle of the night and couldn't seem to relax enough to return to sleep. She got up and looked at her notes again. The question of who followed her car bothered her. She returned to bed and stared at the ceiling, resting on three pillows propping her up and forcing her to stay awake. *Where was the lodger?*

Sixteen

Donna's husband, Tom, lay on the cot of his cell at the county jail deciding if he wanted to bail himself out. The judge had set bail high as it was a murder case, and his resources were limited due to Donna's extravagances and recent lack of interest in the B & B and low bookings.

Maybe, he thought, *it would be good for me to just stay here and think how I got into this situation and how I can get out. I despise the sheriff, such a dandy. He is of no use to anyone and a former or current playmate for Donna. How had it started?*

He tried to remember the early days when, tired of the stress of his stock brokerage job in San Francisco, he took himself up the California coast for a vacation. He drove all the way up Highway One, a long, arduous but spectacular drive on a two-lane road hugging the cliffs of the Pacific Ocean. Dangerously beautiful.

When he came to Mendocino, he had a cold beer at the old hotel and then walked around the small village admiring the old water towers and quaint architecture of the town. He stayed a couple of days. Then the bartender told him of the B &Bs nearby and said he might be more comfortable staying at one for a longer visit. Despite all the romantic couples staying there, the inns had great breakfasts and more comfortable beds, which he could enjoy.

The bartender recommended one owned by a younger person like himself, who was very attractive. She came often to the hotel and had grown up in Mendocino. Her widowed mother had recently passed away and the woman had inherited the property.

He visited the B & B and paid for a week. The owner was indeed vivacious, with her long, blonde hair falling on her shoulders, which she swept back when she laughed, which was often. Not shy at all, she took to him instantly and showed him all the secret spots around town, the best views of the ocean, the best beaches and trails. Within the week, he had grown to love the town and the woman who captured his imagination. She and the wild coast seemed suited for each other.

And so he stayed, sold his apartment in San Francisco, quit his job, and with all the exciting promise of a new venture, he married her with mutual plans of adding a restaurant and buying property for a small winery. He also wanted to build a small house of their own on the cliffs.

Such promise and high hopes only lasted about a year. He learned Donna became bored very easily and all their plans dissolved from neglect. It was soon evident that life was coming to a dull routine of maintaining the current status of the B & B. It also became evident that Donna enjoyed going into town and drinking at the bars.

Her laughter became harsher, more strident and irritable, especially when she had been drinking. Over the last few months, Donna had taken to flirting more openly with any man that was around. They had huge fights over the problems, and Donna showed no signs of stopping. The final argument occurred the night of the B & B association dinner at the hotel. Donna had taken it too far. Not only had she gotten drunk, but she was particularly obnoxious at the dinner table. When he used the bathroom at the hotel, he overheard something that really offended him.

As he entered the bathroom, two men from the tables were talking.

"She is a looker, that one," said one of the men.

"Yeah, and quite a good figure," said the other. "The sheriff took notice. He has been seen with her at least a couple of times."

"I heard she swings both ways," said the first.

"Donna really gets around, even with a woman," whispered the second man and then he noticed Tom closing the door as he entered the bathroom.

Tom couldn't hear all the conversation, but he caught enough to be angry when he heard his wife's name.

"Are you talking about my wife?" he shouted at them.

They both looked startled, not realizing they were talking so loudly.

"We were talking about the new owner of the jewelry store in town," said one.

"I heard you mention my wife's name," he said.

Caught, the two were speechless and trapped in the small bathroom with an angry husband. All three had been drinking.

"We were just repeating a rumor...about a bi-sexual woman... something new in our town."

"Are you saying my wife is involved with this woman?" Tom asked.

"Just a rumor, man, just a rumor," said the other as he pushed his way past Tom.

The other man quickly followed and left Tom alone.

When he came out, Tom went back to the table. Many from the group were leaving and two couples were saying their goodbyes at the front door of the hotel. Tom grabbed Donna by the arm and she reluctantly accompanied him out to the car, which was parked away from the door.

"Now you've taken it too far," said Tom. "What's this about you and a woman? Isn't it bad enough you have been flirting with every man in town?"

"Not just flirting baby, I've been doing the deed and it was fun. More fun than with you, that's for sure. Doing it with a woman is new even for me, but great, more intimate, more romantic."

Tom slapped her in the face. "You are such a bitch," he said. "You are dead to me—dead. Do you hear me?"

"You already have little life in you," she said, freeing herself and walking back indoors to the bar.

Tom got in his car and drove off with the tires squealing. His anger was palpable, and although two couples who witnessed the event hadn't heard every word, they did hear him say, "You are dead to me."

Seventeen

The next morning when the housekeeper appeared early, she was surprised to see they were all awake and dressed. "Up early, I see."

She said that a little too cheerfully, Laura thought.

"I feel better since the lodger has left," Mrs. Evans added.

"He really hasn't left," said June. "His one suitcase is still here."

And I would love to investigate it, thought Laura, but restrained from saying so. Her head still hurt from 'the accident.'

"What's everyone doing today?" she asked. "Are you leaving today, Laura?"

"Not today, but perhaps tomorrow or the next day, according to the doctor."

"She can't be driving yet," said June. "But we should get out of this house, at least for a little while."

Laura did not relish the idea of driving anywhere, not just yet. The phone rang, and all were startled since it rang so little these days. It was a potential guest, who had read one of their few ads in a travel magazine inquiring about a possible visit. Did they have any vacancies? *They sure did*, thought Laura. She excused herself to the kitchen for another cup of decaffeinated tea as the doctor had said to lay off coffee and liquor as well. She poured a cup and returned to the living room where only Stan and June remained.

"Your car is at the auto shop in town," said June. "And before you get all upset about it, it was the only choice at the time. There isn't another car repair shop in at least fifty miles."

Laura winced at the thought of her sports car in the hands of Larry, and having to pick it up at some time.

"Stan volunteered to go with me to see how the repairs are going. A phone call is not enough for him. He wants to meet this man who everyone in town considers creepy," she said.

Laura didn't like the idea of staying at the inn alone, but it seemed a better idea than driving to town and visiting the auto repair shop. "Okay, thanks...both of you. The housekeeper will keep me company until she leaves and then I'll carry my cell phone with me, even on the porch," she said.

After Stan and June left the inn, Laura chatted with the housekeeper, who really didn't appreciate having Laura as her only company. Before lunchtime, she also went out. Laura snacked on some things the Mrs. Evans had made for her but increasingly became restless when Stan and June did not return right away. Her cell phone buzzed in her jeans' pocket. When she looked at the number, she realized it was her soon-to-be-ex-husband.

"Not a good time," she said to him. "I've just been in an accident."

"What happened? Is the car all right?" he asked.

"Interesting you asked about the car first. I'm okay, thanks for asking," she replied, "But I am recovering from a concussion. I don't want to talk with you right now. You're just going to have to wait until I get back to San Francisco. You said you aren't going to marry your lover right away, anyhow, so you'll just have to wait."

True to form, she thought, and with just the press of her index finger, she ended the call before he could say anything. She liked that gesture. She put the phone in her pocket and walked outside to the backyard garden. There was a narrow, worn path leading away from the inn. She decided to walk along the path and see where it led. There were a few small, scraggly trees along the way and Laura really didn't see anything worth looking at. It was turning into a longer walk than she wanted, and she was about to turn back when she strolled into a clearing and spotted a building in the near distance. It was the old barn she and Julie had discovered.

Apparently, the narrow road where she had seen the car that was following her turn off that first night looped around and curved back to the barn. It was shocking to discover that road as well as the walking path from the inn connected to the same barn. Suddenly her hands felt cold and her temple throbbed. Laura did not feel compelled to walk any further and turned around.

Who else knew about this path? Feeling less secure than before, she quickened her steps back to the inn and called Julie on her cell phone in the privacy of her bedroom just in case someone came back.

"Guess what I found?" she asked.

"Don't tell me you went back to the barn after all that's happened?" Julie asked.

"Not intentionally. No. I was walking in the back of the inn and found a narrow path which, when I followed it to the end, led directly to the barn," she said.

"Oh no. Did you tell Stan and June?" she asked.

"They went into the village to check on my car and I stayed here," Laura said. "I wish I hadn't found it. Should I tell them when they get back? Should I tell the sheriff? I don't know what to do. I have been such a burden to all of you." With that last remark, Laura started sobbing.

"It's not your fault, but we need to stop snooping and let the authorities handle this," said Julie. "If the sheriff is involved, he eventually will be found out."

"What's happening in town?" she asked.

"Not much. The locals remain on edge, all with suspicions of their own. The main suspect seems to be Donna's husband, Tom Reynolds, although the evidence seems scarce. The notes the sheriff found at Donna's house are being checked against her own printing and others, including her husband. I'm glad Stan and June are checking on your car because the local teenagers are thinking Larry is involved. To make matters worse, your lodger is still missing, and everyone suspects foul play. The hotel bar has been busier than usual lately, and folks are talking a lot about what has happened and developing theories."

"Seems like you and I helped stir the pot," Laura said.

"That we did," replied Julie.

After she ended her call, Laura made the decision to tell Stan and June about the path when they got home and not to call the sheriff before they arrived. She felt that Stan would not like Clark hearing about it before he did.

What a mess, Laura thought and went into the kitchen to pour herself a glass of wine, despite the doctor's warning. She needed it! When she heard a car driving up the front of the inn, she carried her glass to the front door, only to see the lodger arrive. What should she do? Run out and up the path that led to the barn? That wasn't a great idea. The only other exit was the front door and the lodger was approaching. He didn't seem that threatening as he walked up to the door, so Laura decided to brave it out.

"Good afternoon," she said as nonchalantly as she could manage.

He grumbled an acknowledgment and brushed her aside, heading for his room.

"Where have you been?" she asked. "We were worried about you."

He turned and answered. "I needed to resolve some things and stayed with a friend. I didn't think anyone would worry about me."

"Well...with all that's going on, we did worry," she replied.

"Sorry about that," he said and continued to his room.

After all, thought Laura, *it isn't my inn and I don't have the authority to question him.* After he closed the door, she called Jim Clark.

"I thought you might want to know the missing lodger has returned unharmed," she said.

"Where has he been, and what has he been up to?" Clark asked.

"I didn't think it was my place to ask."

"Really. Nothing much has stopped you before," he barked.

She ignored his remark and simply asked, "If you come to question him, please do not tell Stan that I called you. He already thinks I am too involved."

"So do I, but thanks for telling me. I'll be right there."

When Clark arrived, he went directly to the lodger's room. The man let the sheriff in without any hesitation, but shortly after that, Laura heard them arguing loudly. She could only make out a few words.

"Why didn't you tell me earlier?" demanded the sheriff.

"Not your business!" yelled the lodger.

Laura felt divided, trying not to listen to the conversation and yet curious about what they were saying. She was so absorbed she didn't hear the front door open and Stan and June come up behind her. Laura told them about the sheriff being there to question the missing lodger. The two men emerged from the room with the sheriff leading the way.

"Are you arresting him?" asked Stan.

"No," said the sheriff. "I'm just taking him to my office for more questioning. I can't talk to you about it yet." And they left in the sheriff's car.

"Just like him," muttered Stan. "No information. Big play on his part. How did Clark know he had returned? Did you call him, Laura?"

"Yes I did, Stan. I was here alone with him! I was worried and you two weren't here. I thought the sheriff needed to know."

"You take a lot upon yourself," he shouted. "This is my house and I wish you would have waited until we returned. Maybe we would know more. I could have questioned the lodger myself."

"I didn't think it was wise to wait to call the sheriff. I was frightened," said Laura.

"It wasn't your decision to make!" yelled Stan.

June was silent. It was clear she was not going to interfere. Laura decided it was time to leave. "I think I have overstayed my welcome. Perhaps I should stay at the hotel until I leave," she said, and withdrew into her bedroom to pack.

June followed after her friend.

"I am sorry. Stan has been under a lot of pressure. He should have been more understanding. Please forgive him."

Laura just shook her head. "I think it's best that I leave here this afternoon. My staying just irritates Stan. Julie can watch over me while I'm at the hotel. She lives close by anyway, just north of the village."

"I am sorry it has to end this way. I really need someone to talk with. We had so little time to talk. Please call me," said June.

"I will," replied Laura.

Eighteen

Laura requested a room in the old hotel itself. The rooms were original, from the late 1800s. They were tiny and featured shared bathrooms, which annoyed some guests. The hotel acquired additional space by buying up small adjoining houses nearby and converting them into more rooms for guests. But Laura loved the flavor of the old hotel and its bedrooms with Victorian-style wallpaper and furnishings. She would adjust to the shared bathroom for the privilege of being in the authentic location.

The bedrooms were all upstairs in the style of a boarding house with all of them lined up in a row across from each other. Just up a creaky staircase from the hotel lobby, the narrow steps were a challenge if you carried your own suitcases, but Laura traveled light and wasn't worried about that. Jim Clark called and invited her to have dinner with him, but she declined. Instead, she wore her long Victorian dress to dine by herself in the cozy lobby with a glass of wine and a small salad. Her appetite was dampened by her "accident." Even the warm fire and the quiet, darkened atmosphere of the cozy room did little to ease her mind.

In her bed shortly before nine o'clock, Laura found it difficult to fall asleep. The disturbing events of the past few days scattered in her mind like vignettes in a movie. She pondered the people she had met and possible suspects. Laura couldn't seem to come to any conclusion about the mystery of Donna's secret lover. She heard other guests open and close their doors near her and was relieved when the sounds ebbed at midnight. She was wide awake and wished she could take a walk outside, but she knew that was not a good idea.

Laura got up to use the restroom and peeked out the window at the street below. It was empty, but a late night breeze was blowing through the trees. She wished she could call June or Julie but thought it a bad idea at that time of night. The moon shone down brightly through a cloudless sky and illuminated the parked cars and the buildings on the headlands. *I wonder what the sheriff is doing tonight.* The hotel manager told her earlier someone was always nearby the reception desk. That thought lessened her anxiety, but the silence of the empty lobby and restaurant invaded her thoughts. She pictured a shadowy figure walking quietly up the narrow stairs to the second floor.

Laura shook her head to toss off those thoughts and returned to bed. She lay back on its assortment of fussy pillows and tossed all but one onto a nearby chair. *Who was walking with Donna on that beach?* She pictured Larry sneaking up to confront her. In her next scenario, she pictured the sheriff meeting up with her as planned. In her last vision, she clearly saw Donna's angry husband arguing with her, losing control, and killing her. Laura couldn't sleep and finally got up, dressed in leggings and a sweater and went downstairs to the bar, which would still be open at that hour. There was no one there except Eric, the young bartender who worked part-time. When he asked what she wanted, she let him decide, hoping he could offer something to help her sleep.

"How about Drambuie and soda? It's light and may take the edge off your anxiety. I heard you've had quite a time lately," he commented.

"Yes, I had what some call an accident and what I think was a deliberate attempt to force me off the road," she said. "I'm still scared, but the sheriff doesn't seem to take it very seriously."

"I would be frightened too. Well, you're safe here. Nobody here tonight except me," he said.

After a few sips of her drink, Laura got up the courage to ask the young man some questions.

"What was Donna like?" she asked.

"I noticed she was getting more and more aggressive in her drinking. She had a fight with the sheriff one night and one with her husband after a big dinner party. She flirted with everyone, including me. Her husband probably killed her. He is in the county jail, if you hadn't heard. I think he just got tired of all the drinking and the abuse she poured on him," he added.

Eric looked at her with a frown and continued, "I probably shouldn't be telling you all this," he said. "Why do you want to know?"

"I can't go to sleep wondering who tried to force me off the road. Have you seen an older white sedan around town? It has one bad headlight. That's the car that tried to send me over a cliff," Laura said.

"No," he said, consoling her. "Have another on the house."

"Thanks anyway, Eric. I think I feel better now and should try and get some sleep if I can." Telling herself she was not in any immediate danger, Laura left the tiny bar and looked around the lobby as she climbed the stairs to her room. She fell on top of the bed and threw the extra blanket on top of her, and soon fell asleep out of exhaustion.

An early morning phone call awakened her. Unused to a land phone, she found the loud intrusion both annoying and predatory. It was only Julie checking on her.

"How did you sleep?" Julie asked. "That was a stupid question. Not well, I am sure. I didn't sleep well either."

"You answered your own question," replied Laura. "I can't stop imagining the scenario of Donna's death. I just don't know who was responsible. Any new ideas?"

"No, not really," replied Julie. "I'll call you if I have anything to report."

Next Jim Clark called. He was unpleasant. "Don't leave the hotel," he barked. "And don't be snooping around. We don't have a report from the Highway Patrol yet. I think yours was an accident, but you need to be cautious." He ended his call without letting Laura tell him again that she didn't think it was an accident. By the time she was dressed, Julie called again.

"Okay, I want you to come to Mimi's," she said softly. "I know you're not supposed to leave the hotel, but it won't hurt to just come down one street for a cup of coffee."

Laura put up a fight. "I don't think I should leave the hotel. As much as I hate complying with the sheriff's demands, I think I should stay here."

"It's daylight, and only a short distance to walk. We'll wait here for you. I promise you it won't take long. Besides, you need some fresh air, and I want you to meet someone," Julie remarked.

Laura did want to walk a little. She needed to escape her confinement if only for a little while. She walked softly out of her room and down the carpeted stairs, noting the hotel receptionist had her back turned, and Laura didn't think the young woman saw her leave. She scurried down the block to Mimi's café all the time wondering who the "surprise person" could be. When she entered Mimi's, she spotted Julie at a table with another woman.

The two were engaged in conversation and looked up at the jingling bell announcing Laura's entrance. The woman looked to be in her forties with mousy brown hair. She wore a very forgettable tan blouse that matched her pants. Laura thought it looked chosen by someone who wanted to blend in rather than attraction attention.

Who could she be?

Laura asked Mimi for a soy latte with no whipped cream at the counter and brought it to the table. As she was sitting down, Julie introduced the woman as Helen Lincoln. When all three were seated, Julie revealed her identity in a simple remark, "Helen is Donna's sister."

After she caught her breath, Laura managed a reply. "I am very sorry for your loss, Helen. I didn't know Donna had a sister. You must be overwhelmed by these events."

"Yes, I am," Helen said with her head lowered. "I just arrived yesterday and am staying at her inn. As you know, Donna's husband is being held at the jail and can't make bail. It is very sad and disturbing to be there in her inn without her. Julie told me about your so-called car accident. You too may be in danger. But I really don't think Tom killed her," she remarked.

"What makes you think he isn't involved?" asked Laura.

"I found her diary and some notes she wrote that the sheriff didn't take. She was seeing someone else. She didn't name him, but they met at the beach at night and even during the day sometimes. She says in the diary the creep who lives above them on the hill was watching, so they tried to keep her lover's identity hidden. But true to my sister's show off nature, I am sorry to say, she would taunt the creep...not a smart idea."

She continued. "The two of you ladies should come to the inn to look over all the stuff left behind. Together, we may be able to figure out the identity of her lover. I admit it still could be Tom who killed her, but I don't think so. He was tired of the flirting and cheating she recorded in her diary and was thinking of leaving her. He didn't like it here anyway and was unhappy."

"Have you told any of this to the sheriff?" asked Julie.

"I don't trust him. Donna doesn't mention the man by name, but he does follow the description of the sheriff, and he certainly seems very interested in women. As you already know, they knew each other growing up here in high school," she related.

I don't trust him either, thought Laura. "We should go," a determined Laura said directly at Julie.

"Oh no," cried Julie. "You are not supposed to leave the hotel at all, and I don't want to get any more involved. Neither should you!"

Donna's husband is in jail and I think he may be involved, thought Laura. *What harm would it do just to look at the notes and the diary? I will come right back.*

"Count me in," uttered Laura as Julie looked on in horror and dismay.

"Count me out!" Julie loudly replied. They said their goodbyes and Julie walked out of the shop back to her office. Laura followed Helen to her car and they drove the few miles to the inn at the mouth of the Navarro River.

Nineteen

Sheriff Jim Clark thought about Laura and the events of the last few days. *That woman can be really annoying. Pretty though, in an innocent sort of way. Takes everything at face value. That's a mistake, especially right now.*

He shuffled the papers on his desk. *Donna could be so annoying,* he thought. *She could make such a big scene at the bar with me. She was trouble, even in high school. Marrying that financial whiz of a guy from San Francisco was a big mistake for both of us. Nothing could hold Donna down for long.*

I tried to reason with her when she insisted we meet at the beach, but she was hell bent to get herself into trouble. I thought by returning here, my life would calm down. Boy, was I wrong.

Clark continued straightening out the paperwork on his desk but finally decided to take a walk so he could think more clearly. He signaled his deputy he was leaving for a while and grabbed his cell phone and showed him he was taking it with him.

"Back shortly," he said as he left, swinging open the front door. The air was crisp and breezy. It was a perfectly beautiful coastal day with the smell of the ocean and the fragrance of the flowers planted all over the village.

"Too bad Donna just couldn't be content with what she had going for her. I'll be relieved when her killer is discovered. She was an accident waiting to happen anyway," he said out loud to himself.

The sheriff nodded at a pedestrian walking on the sidewalk and realized he had been talking to himself aloud. The local businessman addressed him.

"Lots on your mind, Sheriff. Any news?" he asked.

"Not right now," Clark replied. "Soon, hopefully. We are working on it," he said knowing that sounded somewhat silly as he was walking down the street instead of working in his office.

As he passed the man, Jim recalled why he had come back to the village after his divorce.

"This is where I grew up," he said, mumbling out loud as there were no more pedestrians on the sidewalk. "I deserve to be here without a hassle. Donna represented all the reasons I wanted to leave. I'll focus my attention on her husband. He's a reasonable suspect."

He continued, but instead of talking out loud, kept his thoughts to himself. *I have even heard rumors that some people accuse me! I guess because of our history and the argument they witnessed. Heard rumors too about Donna and Roberta being together. That one surprised me. And what about the lodger?*

Clark turned around and walked back to his office.

I know it's not Larry. He's weird, but I think harmless. I could be wrong. For now I need to find out more information about the lodger.

Suddenly, he stopped walking when a new thought entered his mind. *Recently forensics could discover more evidence than in the past. But after all, this was not San Francisco. Probably here they could easily make a mistake.* He was somewhat certain they wouldn't find anything incriminating about him on Donna or at the beach, but he wasn't positive. A new worry.

Twenty

As they drove down the narrow lane to the inn from Highway One, Laura started to have second thoughts about leaving her room at the hotel. She kept her concerns to herself and asked no more questions on their way to the inn. When Helen parked her car in front of the house, Laura followed her silently up the steps to the front door. Laura was alarmed when she noticed someone opening the living room curtains. She started to say something to Helen, when the front door opened before they could even knock. Apparently, someone else was at the inn and had seen them drive up. She had believed Helen was alone at her sister's house. *Why would anyone else be there?* She was even more fearful when she recognized the man who opened the door.

It was the lodger from Stan and June's B &B.

Laura recoiled in fear. She screamed and turned to run, when the man held up both his hands and called out, "Sorry I frightened you. I guess by your reaction Helen neglected to tell you I was here. I should have told you earlier. My name is Robert, and I am Helen and

Donna's brother. I came here a while ago to check on Donna without her knowing it. I was worried about her. She has always been a little on the wild side, and her texts led me to believe she was straying from her marriage. I was trying to be big brother, yet anonymous, and that's why I was only watching. I wish now I had talked with her. I regret that I didn't get to see and talk with her before her death."

Laura calmed down, and the three of them hurried inside. They sat around the living room table. There was plenty of room to spread out...the reservations at the inn had been cancelled due to Donna's death and her husband's incarceration. The piles of written material were already sorted by categories Donna and her brother had devised, but they had not reached a definite conclusion. They were desperately trying to find a suspect among the papers.

For two hours, the three of them read through most of the handwritten notes Donna had left behind. They focused on any descriptions or details that might lead them to the person responsible. They read phrases Donna had written in her diary such as, "He doesn't make me happy, but I am really attracted to him. He doesn't seem happy either. We meet on the beach. That's when I am happiest, but one day he struck me. I should get out of the relationship, but I am in too deep. He lives so close I can't really get away."

Other comments included, "I am playing with fire on many counts. I have started a relationship with a woman in town."

At this comment, Donna's brother winced. "She was really spreading herself thin." He sighed. "I should have spoken with her. I will regret it the rest of my life. Maybe I could have helped her."

His sister patted his back and reassured him that was not the case, but Laura thought, *he could be right.*

Nothing was dated the day of her death, but the day before she had written, "We meet tomorrow and I am going to confront our situation. It is getting out of hand. I know I am being a bitch, but I can't stop myself." She drew a picture of the coastline without people, but ironically drew lots of driftwood and kelp.

All beaches near Mendocino are similar, thought Laura, but all three of them agreed it could be the beach where Donna was killed. Chills ran down her spine as Laura touched the picture. Most significant was a comment made after the fight in front of the hotel. The diary, which was not kept daily as further evidence of Donna's scattered life, referred to her husband often with comments like, "Tom was fun at first, but lately he is just a drag. He doesn't want to go with me to the bar in town. I am embarrassing him. I can't help myself. I am happiest when having a good time. We fight almost daily now. I am not afraid of him, but he has gotten physical with me. I push Tom too hard, but he always comes back for more. He thinks he can change me. Good luck with that happening!"

Most significant was a comment made after the fight in front of the hotel after the B & B owners' dinner. Laura related the event to them as she had heard it from Julie. The comment was, "Wow! Tom is really mad at me. This may be a turning point."

Another one caught their attention. "She is only a fling. I need to tell her. She is too intense."

At this point, Donna's brother could not read anymore. "I guess we should take this to the sheriff," he said.

"But was the sheriff involved with her?" Laura asked.

Helen thought for a moment before replying.

"Well, I know I don't trust Jim Clark," Helen confided. "My sister was his steady girlfriend in high school. They were always together as a couple, and she was very upset when he moved away and married. I wouldn't be surprised if they saw each other when he returned. My brother says he is quite the ladies' man."

"I don't trust him either," said Robert. "I talked with him back at Stan and June's inn when Laura didn't know my identity. I told him who I was, and he didn't mention my identity to you, did he, Laura?"

"It would have relieved my mind greatly if I had known who you were," Laura said. "The sheriff didn't seem too worried about Donna's disappearance at first, and then later he acted strangely. He discounted my so-called accident and wants me to leave town. I don't think he would appreciate our alliance. After all, he already took some notes he found here."

Donna's brother related his sightings at the beach. Although he had witnessed Donna's liaisons there during the day, he was too far away on a hill with his binoculars to see who she was with at the time.

Her companion wore hooded jackets and sweat pants, and Robert never really saw their faces, much less knew whether the person he witnessed with Donna was a man or a woman. He never went to the beach at night.

"I have been no help," he lamented. "All I did was look. I spotted Larry watching from his porch, however, many times. He watched the teenagers on the beach as well as Donna. Both taunted Larry, but Donna revealed herself many times. It was difficult for me to see. Could it have been Larry that killed her?"

"I didn't see him on the beach, but then he could have come down that night to settle the score with her."

"We are no further in learning the person's identity than when we started," said Helen.

"You're right," agreed Laura. "It's up to you, of course, whether you want to show all this to the sheriff."

Helen and her brother looked at each other. No words passed between them, but Laura thought, *They are more alike than their sister.*

"We will wait," Robert said. "After all, the sheriff has Tom in custody."

Finally, Laura decided it was time to go back to the hotel. They had exhausted themselves with very little to show for it. They agreed to keep their findings secret, as none of them trusted Clark. All three drove back in Helen's car.

When Laura was dropped off at the hotel, she had the two leave her in front where she waited outside until a couple of tourists parked their car and brought their suitcases in. Laura didn't want the staff to know she had left the hotel. They might report her leaving to the sheriff. Laura peeked inside past the lobby to the receptionist's desk, and when she was certain the receptionist was busy checking them in, she slipped past them onto the narrow, carpeted staircase leading up to the second floor of bedrooms. Once inside her room, Laura relaxed, certain she hadn't been noticed.

It is time for me to go home. I can do no more, and I am putting myself in danger, she thought. So she packed her belongings and checked out of the hotel. Laura supposed they were glad to see her leave, although the receptionist smiled broadly when she checked her out.

"Thanks for staying with us. We hope you will return again soon," she said. *I think that is the standard line. They probably are glad to see me leave. I have caused them nothing but trouble,* thought Laura.

Laura summoned her courage and walked to Larry's auto shop. Thankfully he was not there, and Laura filled out the necessary paperwork and left. She called the sheriff from her car, assuring him she was leaving town.

"You are finally going home," he remarked curtly. "Drive safely on the road this time," he added in an ironic comment.

"Yes, I will," Laura replied.

"Certainly have been at the center of things," he remarked coolly. "Don't let me delay you from going."

She let his comment slide. After ending the call with a forced polite phrase, Laura phoned June, but Stan answered. He was happy to hear her news of leaving as well.

"June is not at home," he said. "She needed to get away and talk with someone. I got tired of listening. Empathy is not one of my strong points."

Certainly not, Laura thought but kept to herself. "Oh, I am sorry to hear that she isn't at home because I wanted to say goodbye. I'll have to call her when I get back." Laura winced at the thought June had to find someone else to talk to, but she needed to be back in San Francisco.

Twenty-one

As Laura was packing her suitcase in her room at the hotel, she had noticed she had left the handmade scarf she purchased in town at the inn. She wanted to retrieve it on her way home. She decided to call Stan again and tell him she would pick it up on her way out of town.

"I would like to stop by and pick up my scarf I left there when I drive back to San Francisco. I'm just leaving the hotel now. Would that be all right?" she asked.

"Oh," he grumbled. "I guess so."

Laura left the hotel and as she put her suitcases in the car, she looked again past the headlands from the view of the hotel on Main Street. Laura thought, *the sheer cliffs are spectacular even from this point of view.* She looked down at the sandy beach and thought, *too bad such tragedy had to happen in beautiful places.* There were clouds overhead and the ocean was calm, not indicative of the drama that had taken place on one of its beaches. *The drive home should at least be pleasant.*

When she arrived at the inn, it looked the same as it had that first day, still empty of cars and guests. She rang the front doorbell, and Stan answered in his usual gruff manner. *No wonder they don't have any guests.*

Stan began the conversation as she entered the inn. "I looked for your scarf, but I couldn't find it in your old room," he said.

"That's because I remembered that I left it in the front room coat closet," Laura replied. She walked across the room and opened the closet door. Then she retrieved it off a hanger.

"Here it is," said Laura. "I'm glad to have it back."

"I didn't think to look there," Stan explained. "Sorry."

Stan looks anxious to have me leave. She walked over to the window looking out into the garden. "Such a beautiful view. I know you want to sell the inn. This garden is a good selling point. I hope you use Julie in the village as your agent," she said.

"June told you about my wanting to sell the inn?"

"Yes, she did. I think she is amenable to that idea now. Oh, there's that path to the barn," Laura said as she looked out the window, changing the subject. "Did you ever go down it?"

Stan's stare followed her. "You are certainly the curious one. Seems like you've been playing quite the detective. Have you learned a lot?" he asked.

"Yes, a lot has happened since I last saw you and June. I met Donna's brother and sister. It turns out your solitary lodger is her brother. He has been staying at Donna's house with their sister, Helen. Now he's spending his time at Donna's inn while Donna's husband, Tom, is in jail."

Stan looked astonished at her remarks. "Really! Well, you have been busy. And what did you learn from them?" he asked.

"Donna kept a diary and in it she talked about several people she was seeing at the beach."

"Several people, huh? Did she happen to mention in the diary who she was seeing?"

"Not by name," Laura answered.

"Have you told the sheriff?" he asked her.

"We decided not to tell him, at least for now since he is holding Donna's husband as a suspect. I know how you feel about the sheriff," she said.

"How do I feel about the sheriff?"

"June said you don't trust him. I guess we don't either."

To her surprise, Stan laughed outright. It was the first time she had heard him laugh since she arrived.

"You are right. I think he may have killed Donna, not her husband, but I could be wrong," he offered. "What else have you learned?"

"Not much, I guess," said Laura. "I still don't know who tried to drive me off the road."

"Perhaps it was an accident," Stan said.

"No, it wasn't," Laura insisted. "That same car that tailgated me the first night I was here tried to drive me off the cliff. I know it for a fact. The Highway Patrol is still investigating the so-called accident."

Stan was silent for a few moments and Laura thought, *I think he is through talking with me.*

"I guess you'll forget about all this when you get home," he said.

"Not really. I have a friend whose husband is a private detective. I think he'll be curious too. And I want to keep in touch with June and Julie. Guess I am like a dog with a bone. I can't quite figure it out and it bothers me. I'll be safely away from this place, however."

"Well, I was curious too. I didn't want to admit it, but I did walk down to the barn. I took that path and the car is there just as you said. Since you are so curious, do you want to see it?" he asked.

Laura hesitated. After all, she was on her way home and it was still too early to be driving back to San Francisco. She would make better time if she left now, but she would like to see the car.

"If you don't, I understand," he continued. "You could just leave all of this behind and forget it."

"I guess I really am nosy," Laura said. "I guess I could spare the time. I'm in no rush."

She followed as Stan walked to the back door. He led her on the narrow dirt path to the weathered barn. They didn't talk anymore on the way. The rusty latch creaked as Stan opened the door. There inside, sitting quietly without any cover, was the car Laura had seen tailgating behind her the first night she arrived. Next to it, to Laura's surprise, stood June.

"Why are you here? I thought you were visiting a friend," asked Laura.

"Waiting to see if you would come out here," June answered calmly. Laura thought *her voice seems distant and detached.*

"Have you told Clark about the car yet?" Stan asked Laura.

"Yes, but he wasn't really interested. The sheriff has Donna's husband in jail, and after all, there is no proof this car really matters. I know someone tried to push me off the road in that car, though, and I don't think it was Donna's husband. Do you know who the car belongs to? Does it belong to Larry?"

"No, it doesn't," Stan replied quietly, in somewhat the same tone of voice as June.

"Who owns it then?" she asked.

"Me," Stan replied, grinning at her. "You shouldn't have been so curious about it, and now you will pay for all your meddling. You've made my life more complicated than it should have been since the accident."

"What accident?" Laura asked.

"Donna's accident?" he said.

"Are you saying it was an accident?" she asked incredulously. *Oh my God,* she thought, *I don't know where he is going with this conversation, but I don't like it. I need to get out of here.*

"You just couldn't leave it alone," he said. "Why did you have to keep poking around when it was none of your business?"

I don't know, thought Laura. *I certainly should have minded my own business. Keep him talking, keep him talking. He probably won't do anything as long as we are talking.*

"How long has June been involved?" she asked Stan.

"You can ask me directly," June said, and Laura turned her attention to her friend. "I only learned of the accident since you and I had our little talk," said June in her own defense. "I confronted Stan and he told me everything—how Donna seduced him and how she taunted him. At first, I was angry and hurt, but I have forgiven him for the affair and the accident. Too bad you just couldn't stay out of it!"

"So it was an accident?" asked Laura. "Then you have nothing to fear with the law," said Laura, hoping they might believe her." *It was no accident*, Laura thought.

"I don't think they will believe me," said Stan. "I swung too hard and when she fell onto the beach, I knew she was dead."

"So you were the one who tried to push me off the cliff in my car?" questioned-Laura.

"Of course it was me. And the investigation of the accident has not yet proven you were telling the truth about that. You're a bad driver and are going to complete your driving record with another crash. It should be easier this time."

"June," Laura pleaded, "don't you see how crazy this all is? You shouldn't get involved." As soon as she said that, Laura thought to herself, *not a good way to win June over with Stan standing here. I have got to get out of the barn. No one knows I have stopped by to get my scarf.*

Laura had her back to the still partially opened barn door. As they talked, she inched her way closer to the door. *How can I distract them for a few seconds so I can turn around and run?* Laura started to wail and sob uncontrollably and then she fell back against the door, becoming even more hysterical. Both Stan and June reacted slowly at first, looking at each other as if to decide what to do. Stan looked at June to confer and with only seconds to spare, Laura spun around and ran out of the barn, but not down the path back to the house.

She ran through the scrubby bushes scattered over the field toward the highway. She weaved back and forth through them, trying to make it difficult for anyone to follow her. Fear built up in her mind like a rising storm, and she could hear her heart pounding. Her head hurt badly, and her legs felt heavy. *No one knows I am there, she reminded herself.* She was alone in her fear.

She could hear and see Stan in the car chasing alongside her on the narrow road and felt someone running after her. It was probably June. She knew Laura would be headed toward the highway for help and it was the direction June was headed after her.

Fear driven, Laura kept running until she fell over a large fallen tree branch. She went down on the ground hard, and immediately put her hand across her mouth to keep from crying out with pain. Her knee was badly scraped and blood was oozing out of the wound, trailing down her leg. Her knee was beginning to swell. Laura picked herself up from the rough ground and continued running, but she was limping and slowing down. She could hear Stan's car turn around and head back toward her, but the running behind her had stopped.

Did June quit running after me and get in Stan's car? she asked herself, *or has she stopped near me.* Finally Laura came across the backyard of a neighbor's house, but when she knocked at the back door, no one answered. It looked locked up and empty. Julie had told her how many people bought these houses as second homes and were away most of the time. She sat on the stoop of the house for a moment, retrieved her cell phone from her pocket and called Julie for help. Someone needed to know her location.

"Good morning," Julie responded cheerfully. "It's another beautiful day in Mendocino. Fine time it is to look at property here. We have lots to choose from, including property in the country as well as the village itself."

"Julie...it's Laura. I am at Stan and June's inn. Stan is chasing me with his car and June is chasing me by foot. Stan admitted he owns the car that tried to knock me off the road. It's the same car we found in the barn. June is with him. She seems to be complicit. He is the one who killed Donna, although he told June it was an accident. I don't believe him, but apparently, he has convinced her somehow. Stan said I was to have another accident in my car. I am terrified and keeping ahead of them the best I can, but I fell and am hurt. I don't know what to do. I need help right now!" she cried.

"Oh my God...I don't know what to tell you. The sheriff just came by and told me he released Donna's husband, Tom, from jail earlier today. He says he doesn't have enough evidence to hold him and he suspects someone else. I'll try to reach him," Julie replied. "I'll call nine-one-one too!"

Laura ended her call and listened to the sounds around her. She could no longer hear Stan's car. For all she knew, the two of them could be right behind her. Panicked, she knew she didn't dare stop. When she tried to get up, her leg gave way at the knee. She was hurt worse than she had originally thought.

She looked around at her surroundings and discovered an old cellar door just near the stoop. She limped toward it and leaning over, groped around and found it was unlocked. She opened both of the narrow wooden doors leading to the basement as quietly as she could. She walked down the steps and closed the doors behind her. Laura was reluctant to enter the basement, as it was dark and confining.

If he is behind me, I will be trapped in here. What will he do if he discovers me hiding? But I don't have any other good options.

Suddenly she could hear footsteps again, slower but getting closer by the minute. They seemed quite heavy. *Those footsteps must be Stan's.* Reluctantly, she went down the steps as quietly as she could, enduring the pain at each rung. At the bottom, she stood frozen with fear. Her head was still throbbing, and perspiration was streaming down her forehead. She wiped it away with her hand, so she could see better. She realized her whole body was shaking, and it was not just from the cold. She didn't dare use the bright light on her cell phone. *He'll see it,* she thought.

Then she heard only one set of footsteps. *They have separated to look for me.* Laura could hear the crunching of the dry leaves as whoever it was moved around the house. He was searching for her. The sound came closer.

Oh God, he is opening the doors to see if I came down here.

Feeling her way in the dark, Laura worked her way toward the back of the cellar, moving as silently as she could. She hunched down behind a large, dusty barrel and waited in terror.

She waited but couldn't hear the footsteps anymore. But she was certain he would not give up his search. Minutes seemed like hours and the old dark cellar became her prison. It was pitch black in the back of the cellar, and the only light she could see was coming from slits in the old doors.

She scrunched up even smaller behind an old wooden barrel. A large, bedraggled rat crossed slowly directly in front of her. The movement startled her, and she couldn't prevent an involuntary scream. *That is not good,* Laura thought. *Now Stan will know I'm inside. I am going to die here in this dark cellar.* She could smell the rancid air of the basement and see the cobwebs hanging from the dusty ceiling and walls.

This is where my life will end. It is too late for me. He is here, she thought, and Laura started to cry.

Twenty-two

"Laura. Laura. Are you in there?" The sound of a male voice chilled her.

"Who is it?"

"It's me...Jim Clark."

"Is it really you?" she shouted back. *Even now I can't keep my mouth shut!* she thought.

"Really, Laura," he called.

"Why should I believe you? How do I know it's really you and not Stan?" yelled Laura.

"Believe me," he shouted back. "You have to. You don't really have a choice. I was on my way from checking out the barn and the car with Larry when Julie called."

Laura watched as the twin doors of the basement entrance began to open. When she couldn't recognize the dark silhouette of the man standing at the top of the steps, hysteria engulfed her. She knew her life had come down to this.

Clark raced down into the basement and gathered her up. Laura struggled, fighting with him, fear tearing at her mind. She still was not convinced it was a person she could trust.

"Shush, Laura, shh—listen to me. I'm here. I have you. You're safe." The sheriff clamped his arms around her, struggling to overcome her fear.

Laura finally recognized his voice. She could hardly breathe. "Stan is chasing me. June too! They are both involved in Donna's death."

"I thought it might just be Stan. But just before Julie called, I had talked with Larry about the car—the one you had seen the first night—and the one you said tried to drive you off the cliff. I believe you now." He was caressing her hair until she stopped fighting him.

"You know, woman, you really do have a wild imagination, though, you must admit!"

Laura was still struggling to catch her breath. "They both were after me! Where are Stan and June now?" Laura asked, still shaking with fear.

"I have them both safely handcuffed outside. I've called in for backup. Are *you* all right?" He could feel her relaxing. "Are you all right?" he asked again while loosening his grip.

"I have Stan in my patrol car and June is handcuffed to the door of the other side. I don't want them talking with each other. Stan is silently staring out the car window and June is protesting loudly that she had nothing to do with Donna's death. She claims Stan made her chase after you, but I can't take a chance at this point until I hear the whole story. I will take the consequences later if I'm wrong about her," he said.

"Your story of the car following you on the first night you came, and your crash got me thinking. I checked with Larry to see if he had fixed a car with a bad headlight. He told me he had replaced the headlight on Stan's car and that Stan stored it in his barn. I don't know about June's involvement. That would surprise me. Was she chasing you too?" he asked. "Everyone thought she was so nice!"

"So did I!" said Laura, who was still shivering with fear. "I forgot the scarf I bought in the village and remembered when I started to leave town to drive to San Francisco. So I called June to say I would stop by on my way out of town to say goodbye…and retrieve my scarf.

"Stan said June was visiting friends. When I arrived at the inn for my scarf, Stan and I talked for a few minutes and then we went to the barn. He told me he had found the car there. When we went in, June was standing next to the car. I was surprised to see her there instead away visiting friends. It was then she told me that Stan had confessed everything to her. He said he had an affair and that Donna's death was an accident. Donna said she believed his story. But they intended to kill me!"

The sheriff realized she was going into shock. He had to keep her mind busy till the ambulance arrived. So he said, "Well, it was no accident. The coroner said the blow was hard and from above. Donna couldn't have taken such a blow falling. I'm sorry I didn't believe you earlier…about anything," Clark said. "I know I was harsh, but you do meddle!"

Laura pulled away from him. "June is involved. She said so. If only after the fact. Don't believe her about not knowing. I think she may have been chasing me, too, although I couldn't see her. I barely got away from them in the barn. Otherwise, I probably wouldn't be alive now. I can't believe I'm safe. Did Julie call you?" asked Laura.

"Yes, she was hysterical too," he said. "She wants you to either go to the hospital in Fort Bragg or when the emergency personnel check you out and say it's okay, you can stay with her tonight. You can't drive back to San Francisco today."

He is always telling me what to do, thought Laura. "Good thing I got away from both of them." She spit the words out as if they were venom.

He looked her in the eye. "Is it possible you could give me just a little credit? As I said, I left instructions to let Donna's husband out of jail. I discovered information about the car and the barn from Larry."

"Well, I do appreciate your finding me," said Laura, feeling more composed.

It took you long enough to suspect someone other than Donna's husband. After all, you were a suspect in many people's minds, but as it turns out, it was a good thing it was you who found me.

"So it was Stan who tried to drive me over the cliff?" Laura asked.

"We don't have the full report yet, but the Highway Patrol says it does look suspicious. I guess I should have believed you, but you do come up with some wild ideas. You are one lucky lady."

"Luckier than June. What is going to happen to her now?" Laura asked.

"Don't you worry about that. You're safe. I am going to have to straighten this whole mess out. You just worry about feeling better."

Just then two Highway Patrol cars and the ambulance arrived. The sheriff talked with the officers as Laura was checked out by the emergency personnel who addressed and bandaged her wounds. Laura didn't want to go to the hospital and asked for a lift to Julie's house. She would get her car later.

Laura could see Stan and June in separate police cars. Stan just looked down, but June stared down away from Laura. *She does look contrite,* thought Laura. *Well, she should. I guess Stan really got to her. I really thought she was my friend. I guess I didn't really know her as well as I thought.*

"Wait there for me, Laura," the sheriff said. Turning to the officers, he continued giving orders. "One suspect is in my vehicle and the other outside, so they couldn't talk with each other. Could you take them to the county jail for me in separate cars? I will be there shortly to book them both. I need to help Laura."

With Stan and June in two patrol cars, the officers left down the very same narrow dirt road where Stan had been chasing Laura in his car. The ambulance followed behind them without Laura.

The sheriff put her in his passenger's seat and they drove back to town. He still was telling her what to do.

"Stay out of trouble, Laura," he commented. "Maybe you could be content by just reading a good mystery. I must admit, though, it certainly won't be the same here without you and your imagination."

They drove into the village past the dynamic view of the headlands before passing Mendocino going north. It was a beautiful postcard view, and Laura did love the town. She looked fondly at the old water towers and quaint wooden buildings as they drove past the village and up the road to Julie's home. As they approached, Julie ran out to greet them.

"Oh my God," Julie shouted. "You're safe, Laura. I was so worried after you called. I can't believe what I am hearing about Stan and June, especially June. She was always such a sweet person."

"You never know," Clark said. "I hear some people in town thought it could have been me who killed Donna." With that remark he looked directly at Laura.

"There was talk of several suspects," Laura admitted. "Including you."

"We have lots to talk about," said Julie. "I want to know everything."

Julie ushered Laura into her house and asked Clark if he wanted to come in.

"Some other time, Julie. I have lots to do right now. Maybe tomorrow or the next day before Laura drives home, I'll come by, if that's okay."

Julie smiled. "Sounds good. I'll try to keep her here for at least a day. She shouldn't be driving until she settles down. That was quite a scare."

"Things should calm down around here now that Stan and June have been caught. We can return to a peaceful community. Laura can sure stir things up," he commented.

"That's for sure," said Julie. "It won't be the same without her."

As he left to get into his car, the sheriff turned and addressed Laura directly. "If I don't get the chance to see you before you leave, call me sometime."

"Okay," said Laura as she turned to walk inside Julie's house, but she mumbled to herself. *You wish! No way of that ever happening!*

Twenty-three

Laura related the entire story to Julie on the porch as they sat sipping tea. She was exhausted and worn out from her ordeal, but she couldn't think of resting on a bed in a closed bedroom. Finally, Julie suggested that Laura lie out on the comfortable couch in the living room. Julie sat next to Laura and waited for her to fall asleep.

The telephone rang, and Laura thought it odd that Julie still had a land phone but decided the older people in the village probably felt more comfortable with using it instead of a cell phone. Julie quickly answered, but Laura was awake.

After she hung up, Julie said, "Jim Clark called and asked how you are. I told him that he could stop by later in the day to check on you. I hope that was all right?"

I would rather not see him, thought Laura, *but it's too late now.*

"It's okay," she said. "I can't tell you how much I appreciate your taking me in. I didn't want to be in the hospital at Fort Bragg again. I won't stay with you more than a couple of days. You have been so kind to me."

"You stay as long as you like," said Julie.

She is probably one of the only people in town who are what they seem to be!

Julie hurried off to her kitchen to make some more tea and light sandwiches for both of them. Laura lay on the couch, resting comfortably with lots of pillows and a warm quilt, comfortable in her safety while thinking about her close call.

June had said she learned about Stan's involvement while confronting him after she and June talked that day. I told her about discovering the car in the barn with Julie, thought Laura. *June did seem surprised, though.*

Julie returned with a tray of sandwiches and more tea and pulled up the coffee table to place the food in front of Laura.

"Do eat something," she said. "You need to gather some strength, especially before you drive back to San Francisco."

"Why would June help Stan after she learned of his involvement? How could she believe it was an accident? Most importantly, why would she join him in trying to get rid of me? I don't understand," said Laura.

"I don't get it either. She always seemed like such a complacent person, and while she was with us at Mimi's café, always whimpering about her husband and how he hated it here. I didn't know her that well, but that was my impression whenever I saw her," Julie said.

"Now she's saying her husband made her follow after me. I don't believe it for a minute. You should have seen the way she looked at me at the barn. It was a cold look, unlike any expression I had ever seen on her face, including when she would be angry in college," said Laura. "It is as though I have never known her."

"Sometimes people are not what they seem to be," replied Julie calmly. "You probably already figured that out about our little village already. I just heard a story about Sheila, our new jewelry store owner. I heard she too might have been having a fling with Donna. Can you believe that?"

Old news thought Laura, but she didn't say she already knew.

"You are one of the good ones," Laura said to Julie.

"You just met me. Perhaps I was involved too," she said.

Laura just stared at her.

"Just kidding," said Julie and poured some more tea.

Julie's doorbell rang and when she opened the door, Laura saw the sheriff standing there. She thought to herself, *be nice, after all he did save you.*

He brought news Laura didn't like to hear. June was protesting her innocence loudly while Stan was still not talking.

"She understands now that Donna's death was no accident, and she says she was not involved, which I tend to believe. However, that does not clear her of possible charges concerning you," he said.

"What do you mean by possible charges, Jim?" Laura asked.

"She still claims Stan forced her to go after you and be involved. I'm struggling with the idea that version of the story could be true. Probably the courts will have to decide," he said. "Furthermore, she is saying that she wasn't in the barn at all. That you are lying to implicate her," he offered.

Laura thought for a moment and then realized something. Remembering the staring face of June when Laura entered the barn, she realized June was not only standing next to the car, but she was leaning on it.

"Does she say that she didn't know the existence of the car in the barn? Is she denying that?" she asked.

The sheriff looked at her and waited a few seconds to reply. "Yes, she claims she knew nothing about the car and that you never told her about it."

"Gotcha! Better yet, got her!" said Laura. "Her fingerprints will be all over the car because she was leaning on it when I saw her at the barn!"

Clark smiled. "If you ever need a job as a deputy sheriff, you have it. Do go through the training, however, and then come see me. I had better go back and confront her with her statement. Got to think how to phrase my questions to her on the way back to town. Thanks. Give your mind a rest now."

"Sheriff…" Laura addressed his back as he walked to the door. "You don't always have to give me advice, you know."

Clark turned around and smiled again. "I'll try," he said.

Twenty-four

Laura finally left town after two days at Julie's house. She felt ready to drive and was secure in her knowledge that both Stan and June would be prosecuted. Originally, she had been sorry for June, but since June's arrest, Laura decided her sympathy was not warranted. The evening before, she and Jim Clark had dinner again at Café Beaujolais, but this time his manner was less patronizing. *He is really trying*, thought Laura. *I don't know if he can really change, but the evening was far more pleasant than before.*

Laura learned more about his background. It was true that he, Donna, Larry, and some others from town had gone to high school together. He had left, however, and married early in a different town. The marriage hadn't worked out, and he had no children. He decided to become a police officer and had gone through the training only to find himself disheartened in a larger town. So when he looked into other possible jobs, he discovered Mendocino needed a sheriff and he applied.

"I like being back," he said. "In many ways. But in some instances, like this one, I can become too involved as a citizen of the town where I live. Knowing all the people so well, it is difficult to see them any other way than when I meet them in town. Usually the offenses are small, and the job is pretty easy. This incident was big, and I admit I overlooked some things."

Yes, you did, thought Laura, but she was restrained and kept that comment to herself.

"I was certain Donna's husband was guilty and I had tunnel vision. I knew Larry, odd as he is, wasn't a good suspect. But I only learned lately that Sheila had an affair with Donna. I knew Donna was becoming wilder, but that did surprise me."

"I heard you two were quite an item in high school. I also heard she was trying to rekindle your attraction after you returned," Laura said. *Maybe that comment was too personal.*

Jim was quiet for a few moments and then replied, "That's what the fight was about that townspeople witnessed outside the hotel bar. She was coming on strong and I left. Donna was drunk, and I probably should have arrested her for being drunk and disorderly. I did call her husband from my car on the way home to come and get her. No, I wasn't interested anymore. I learned that, after that fight, half the townspeople thought I might have been the one who killed her. Did you?"

"Sorry, I shouldn't have brought it up," Laura said, not answering the question he raised.

"It's okay. I want things to be straight between us," he said and then reached across the small table and touched her arm. "I really do like you and want to see you again. After all, unless they plead guilty, you may have to come back to testify," he said.

I hope that won't be true. Laura let his remark slide without replying but left his hand on her arm. She didn't know if she wanted to become involved with him. As much as she liked this town, her memories included ones that were very unpleasant. She was looking forward to going home and resuming her life. The divorce didn't seem as bad an experience as what she had just been through. She was just beginning to learn to trust her instincts.

If I have to come back, I just might see him in a different light. Who knows?

Meet Joyce Johnson

Joyce lives in a small village in California. A third generation Californian, she enjoys both the beauty and mystery associated with the sea and the unique mountains-to-ocean character of her state.

Works From The Pen Of Joyce Johnson

Highway One - Set in Northern California on the Mendocino coast, it is the story of a young woman who housesits her friend's B & B only to be caught up in a murder.

Final Voyage - Final Voyage takes place on a cruise ship bound for the Southern Caribbean. In this cozy mystery, Corinne becomes entangled in the story behind a young woman's death.

Illusions - Young financial consultant from San Francisco involves himself in the investigation of his friend's death at a cabin in the Sierra Nevada mountains.

Letter to Our Readers

Enjoy this book?

You can make a difference

As an independent publisher, Wings ePress, Inc. does not have the financial clout of the large New York Publishers. We can't afford large magazine spreads or subway posters to tell people about our quality books.

But, we do have something much more effective and powerful than ads. We have a large base of loyal readers.

Honest Reviews help bring the attention of new readers to our books.

If you enjoyed this book, we would appreciate it if you would spend a few minutes posting a review on the site where you purchased this book or on the Wings ePress, Inc. webpages at: https://wingsepress.com/

Visit Our Website

For The Full Inventory
Of Quality Books:

Wings ePress.Inc
https://wingsepress.com/

Quality trade paperbacks and downloads
in multiple formats,
in genres ranging from light romantic comedy
to general fiction and horror.
Wings has something for every reader's taste.
Visit the website, then bookmark it.
We add new titles each month!

Wings ePress Inc.

3000 N. Rock Road

Newton, KS 67114

www.ingramcontent.com/pod-product-compliance
Lightning Source LLC
Chambersburg PA
CBHW070658100726
47907CB00007B/2252